SHOOTER

BROTHERS COURAGEOUS, BOOK 1

VANESSA GRAY BARTAL

DRYCREE PRESS

"knew you were trouble the minute I met you."

"Aw, Lassiter, I bet you say that to all the girls."

"Actually, I do. Which makes it all the weirder you have a girl's name."

"Nothing wrong with my name. Kelsey is a great name."

"Name another dude with it," Nick commanded.

"That old guy who played Frasier on TV. My mom loved that show."

"Okay, that's one. But that guy wasn't a marine," Nick said.

"Neither am I," Kelsey replied. "At least, not yet. What number are we on here?"

"956 last time I checked." Last time he checked it was also three in the morning. They had been doing push-ups and sit ups in sets of a hundred for what seemed like forever. Nick was exhausted, as he knew Kelsey was, but neither of them dared to complain because boot camp wasn't really for someone who couldn't hack a few reps. Then again maybe it wasn't for them anyway. Nick with his rebellious streak and Kelsey with his inappropriate sense of humor and inability to keep his mouth shut didn't fit in.

"This wasn't what I thought when I signed up. Parris Island, you know? The tour guide made it sound so great. *The exclusive part of South Carolina. Very elite.* Then I get here and it's a bunch of guys in camo yelling at me. When this is over, I am so getting a refund," Kelsey said.

Nick laughed and his arms shook, making him precariously close to toppling over. "Shut up, man. You're the reason we're here anyway." They had been on a forced march, standing next to each other, when Kelsey had started muttering Chuck Norris jokes under his breath. Nick laughed out loud, which was a highly inappropriate response to the particularly horrible sentiment their drill instructor had been screaming at the time. And voila here they were, doing hundreds of reps while everyone else was getting sleep—a commodity that had become more precious than almost anything else.

At last they reached a thousand and lay on their backs, their arms and abs a quivering mass of jellylike muscles neither of them would ever cop to. In fact, if their drill instructor came back and asked them if they wanted to do another thousand, they would say "Aye, Sir," with a smile because this was boot camp, and not merely boot camp, but *marine* boot camp. Everyone was looking to be the bravest, toughest, and the best.

"You got a girl, Lassiter?" Kelsey asked.

"I find them when I need them. What about you?"

"I don't want to talk about it. Don't be a nosy parker."

Nick laughed, stifling his groan. "What?"

"I dunno. It's something my grandma used to say whenever I asked questions. What are you going to do after camp?"

"I don't know," Nick said. "I'm not so much into making life plans, you know? I don't even know how I wound up here." He did, actually, but he wasn't telling Kelsey. The two had been inseparable for three weeks, but it was one thing to laugh with someone and another to admit your mistakes and failures to him.

"You know how the sergeant keeps telling us you have to look out for your buddy? That you're only as good as the man standing next to you?"

"Yeah," Nick replied. It was the first time he had heard Kelsey sound even close to serious, so he was wary, waiting for either a punch line or something profound.

"I've been thinking we make a pretty good team. I think we should stick together wherever we go from here."

Nick was humbled. No one had ever wanted to stick with him before. Usually they wanted to dump him off in a cornfield and hurry away before he came to and made more trouble. "That's not really up to us, you know? We could end up anywhere."

"Okay, you're being literal. I didn't mean physically stick together, although that has some merits. I meant be a team, like I got your back and you got mine. 'Cause I gotta tell you, Lassiter, there's no one like that for me now, and being here, I don't know. It makes you think about stuff."

Nick did know. He had been thinking along similar lines the last few weeks. He was eighteen and alone in the world, a fact that hadn't really bothered him until he came to this place that talked about sticking together as if it were the most important thing in the universe. That was great when it came to the corps, but who did he stick to on the outside? No one. And now Kelsey was volunteering to be that person. "Like brothers?" Nick said. Was his voice husky, or was it his imagination? He hoped Kelsey wouldn't notice and point it out.

"Yeah, like brothers," Kelsey said, and his voice sounded a little rough around the edges, too. "Now, your first task as my brother is to drag me inside and stick me in my bunk. If anyone wakes up, you're going to need to come up with a believable story about how I lost the use of my arms and legs because I seriously can't move. Something good that makes me look like a hero. Got that, Lassiter?"

But Nick couldn't answer; he was laughing too hard.

CHAPTER 1

Nine years later...

It was supposed to be a simple coffee run. Nick was dispatched to Starbucks for some frilly concoctions marines would never admit to enjoying because they were supposed to drink coffee that tasted like sludge and say "Thank you, sir, may I have another?" Instead, he and his teammates often used words like "grande," "half-caf," and "extra foam." He was standing in line, third from the front, when the bell over the door dinged, admitting another customer. Nick didn't turn around because why should he? The store was busy, and turning around every time someone entered would have revealed his paranoia. He wasn't happy about the setup, however, not liking to have his back so long exposed as people came and left the store. He talked himself out of constantly turning around by reminding himself he wasn't in the Middle East; he was in Starbucks. Nothing ever happens in Starbucks.

But it was his luck he was there on the one day something actually happened in Starbucks. He had just taken a step forward, making him second in line, when the door tinkled and Nick heard it, the sound of a round being pumped into a chamber. He crouched as he spun, reaching for his weapon and finding it not there. For a second he was confused—the bad guy had a gun, why didn't he? Then he had to remind himself again this was Starbucks and of course he wouldn't have armed himself to retrieve coffee.

In an instant, he realized he was the only person in a defensive crouch. The other customers were turned toward the door in curiosity, easy pickings for the disheveled man holding a sawed-off shotgun. Nick's only consolation was the man was pointing the weapon toward the ceiling and not toward any people. Either he was sorely untrained, or he really didn't want to kill anyone. But if he didn't want to kill anyone, why was he in a Starbucks with a sawed-off shotgun? It was more likely he simply wasn't thinking rationally, either functioning on fractured emotions or a substance now ruling his brain. Nick squinted; the guy's pupils were blown. Whatever he was on, it was now telling him what to do. Nick could only hope his reactions were slow.

Against his instinct, Nick made himself stand and blend in with the other customers. He wished desperately for his ghillie suit, though in order to blend into the scenery here it would have to be covered with tasteful cardboard cups and not its usual burlap and twine. Slowly, Nick began to make himself invisible, blending into the scenery as he inched toward the gunman. If he played it right, he would be beside the man before he even realized he was there, and then he would neutralize him before he could get a shot off. That was the plan. As Nick had learned soon after basic training, however, plans almost never work out.

"Drop your gun." Nick froze, staring at the woman holding a handgun on the man with the shotgun. She was the last person in line, so they were very close together. For one brief shining moment, Nick's heart turned over with the hope she was a police officer who knew what she was doing. Then he took in her amateurish stance and realized she was simply a woman who happened to own a gun, a gun she was now holding as if she had seen one too many episodes of police dramas on television. Nick began creeping toward them again when the man dropped the barrel of the gun, aiming it squarely at the woman's chest. That was when Nick gave up trying to be subtle and leapt, knocking the man to the ground as a shot went off.

It wasn't the shotgun; it was the handgun, and it hit Nick squarely in the behind as he fell to the ground. He had been shot once before, nicked in the upper arm. There was a strong possibility he would be shot again, but that didn't mean it ever felt good. The other patrons screamed and chaos ensued. Nick concentrated on neutralizing the subject, resisting the urge to snap the man's neck entirely. Instead he pressed his thumb on his carotid until he slumped into unconsciousness, his gun falling gently to the floor. Nick reached for the gun, but it was already gone. The woman had picked it up and was now holding in her free hand, making her look like some sort of female Rambo.

"Put. The gun. Down," Nick said in his most serious do-it-or-die tone.

"No," the woman answered. "What if he wakes up and lunges for it? This way he'll have to go through two of us."

Nick stared at her, disbelieving. In his world, people followed orders, especially when it came to guns. Now this woman who had already shot him was standing there with two guns in her hands, defiantly disobeying him.

"He's not getting up any time soon. Now put the guns down before you shoot someone else."

She frowned. "Someone else? What are you talking about?" He watched as the horrible realization registered. "I shot you?" she whispered.

"Yes," he said. His voice was tight because the pain was becoming intense.

The woman set down the guns and turned to the man behind her. "If that guy stirs, I want you to pick these up, okay?" He nodded the same way Nick had expected her to nod when he gave her the order. She knelt in front of Nick.

"Where are you hit?" her tone was that of someone speaking to an invalid.

"I'm fine," Nick said through gritted teeth.

She tipped her head, studying him. "Are you a cop or a soldier?"

"Marine," he said.

"Figures," she said. "Look, I understand you're very brave and very tough, but I also know you're shot and you must be in pain. Tell me where it hurts."

Was she for real? Tell her where it hurts, as if she were his mother. "Look, lady," he began, but she ignored his words and began to search him. It didn't take her long to locate the wound because a bright blossom of blood was spreading across the seat of his pants. Without asking his permission, she reached down and ripped the pants. He screamed when she jerked down his boxer shorts and inspected the wound.

"What are you doing?" he yelled.

"I'm looking at it. What if it hit an artery?"

"There aren't any arteries in the butt," he said. "There's only fat and that's where it's lodged. Will you please pull my pants up?"

She didn't, though. She remained staring at his behind as if considering a purchase. "I think maybe you're right. It's bleeding, but not profusely. Must not have hit an artery."

Nick counted to ten in his head.

"Why do you have a tattoo of a pig?" she gently touched her fingertip to the tattoo over his left cheek.

"None of your business," he ground out, squinching his eyes tightly closed

"But a pig, really? That's an odd choice for a marine."

"I have my reasons, okay? I'm not asking about your tattoos, am I?"

"I don't have any tattoos," she said.

"Really?" She moved to his head and somehow captured his interest so he wasn't thinking about the pain anymore. "Everyone has tattoos."

"I don't," she said.

"Why not?" he asked. Before she could answer, sirens pierced the air and drew closer, halting abruptly outside the coffee shop. Whoever called them must have relayed the fact that the shooter was down because they didn't try to set up a perimeter and take stock of the situation. Instead they streamed in, weapons drawn and aimed at Nick.

"He's the good guy," the woman said. She shifted, shielding his body with hers. "And he's injured. Is an ambulance on the way?"

"One is coming, ma'am. Can you tell me what happened?"

"I sort of accidentally shot him. It all happened very fast."

If Nick weren't in so much pain, he would have laughed at the officer's expression. Clearly the last thing he was expecting to hear was that the small woman on the floor was the shooter. "Is this a domestic situation?" he asked.

"No," she said, and then she began to tell the story of how it all came about.

"Do you have a concealed carry permit?" he asked.

"Yes, I do. It's in my purse." She reached for her purse, but the cop raised his gun.

"Slowly," he commanded. Even though he knew it was probably standard procedure, Nick felt infuriated on her behalf. Did the cop really think Miss Goody Two Shoes No Tattoos was the bad guy?

She moved like molasses as she reached into her purse and held out her concealed carry permit. The officer took it, along with her identification, and called it in to his dispatch, probably to make sure she had no outstanding wants or warrants.

"How are you doing down there, Marine?" she asked, peering down at him.

"I'm fine," he lied. In truth, his tuchus stung so badly he was seeing spots, and the suspect beneath him, who didn't smell so good, was beginning to stir. The officer towering over them noticed that, too. His already high adrenaline kicked into overdrive as he shoved Nick and the woman aside in order to cuff the suspect before he could fully rouse.

"Watch it," the lady yelled, scrambling to try and keep Nick's backside from bouncing on the ground. No such luck, though. He bounced and skidded, gritting his teeth to keep from crying out. The woman crawled over and rolled him onto his stomach, offering instant relief from the pressure.

"Where is that ambulance?" she yelled, so loudly even in the midst of the chaos people stopped what they were doing and turned to give her their attention.

Once the suspect was cuffed, the officer came over and crouched beside them. "Sorry about that, buddy. I forgot you were injured. How you doing?"

Nick didn't answer. He simply glared and tried not to let the stinging tears fill his eyes. They were merely a reaction to the pain, but there would be no way to explain to the onlookers. All they would know was a marine had taken a little pop to the behind and cried like a baby.

The woman, who was turning out to be an all around valuable asset, began to smooth her fingers gently over his forehead. "The ambulance," she prompted the officer.

"It's pulling up now," he assured her. He gave her back her purse. "We'll need you to fill out a statement."

"I'm going to the hospital with him," she said.

Both the officer and Nick protested over that pronouncement, but she held up a hand. "I'm going," she said, steely determination in her tone.

The officer rolled his eyes and went to greet the ambulance. "What's your name?" Nick asked.

"Ashleigh," she replied.

"Are you a marine?" Nick asked.

She laughed and shook her head.

"You should be," he said, and then the paramedics were there, and everything faded to a hazy shade of gray.

CHAPTER 2

*N*ick hadn't expected sympathy from his commanding officer, but he also hadn't expected to receive such a dressing down while lying face down on a gurney, waiting to have a bullet pulled out of his posterior.

"Do you have any idea what you have cost the United States Marine Corps, Corporal?"

"Yes, sir," Nick replied.

"No, I don't believe you do. Because you went and got yourself shot at Starbucks, an entire mission has been scrubbed. An entire mission, Corporal."

"Yes, Sergeant," Nick said as a nurse washed his fanny with Betadyne.

"I don't have to tell you what scrubbing an entire mission means, do I Corporal?"

"No, Sergeant," Nick replied, but to no avail.

"It means people's lives are at stake, to say nothing of how much money is wasted."

"Yes, Sergeant," Nick replied. The screen opened and Nick hoped it was the doctor coming to dig out the bullet, but it wasn't. It was

Ashleigh. He watched in amazement as she pulled up a chair and sat in front of his head.

"Did you hear me, Corporal?"

Nick hadn't heard, but since he guessed it was simply more of the same he replied with, "Yes, Sergeant."

"Good. Now, sore butt or not, you have one week to recover and then you are going on your mission. Is that clear, Corporal?"

"Yes, Sergeant." Nick gritted his teeth, not because of the pain and not because of the ear-chewing he was receiving, but because he was going to be out of commission for an entire week. What was he going to do with himself while he recovered?

"That wasn't your dad, was it?" Ashleigh asked. Nick set the phone on the bed, but she took it and put it in a more secure place on the stand to her right.

"Sort of," Nick said. He was still feeling glum. "What are you doing here?"

"I waited for someone else to come for you, but no one ever did, so I figure I sort of owe it to you to distract you. Rumor is you're refusing general anesthetic for the surgery."

"I have to," Nick blurted.

"Because of your job?" she guessed.

"Yes." He left it at that, glad she didn't ask any more. She seemed to know a lot about being a marine, but then she also seemed to be a local. Anyone living near Camp LeJeune all her life was bound to learn something. "Is your dad a marine?"

"No," she said. She glanced over his shoulder before quickly fastening her eyes on his again. "Sorry, I didn't mean to peek. Movement caught my attention."

"You sort of already saw it when you ripped my pants off," he said.

She blushed, and he smiled. "That wasn't the way you're making it sound."

"Really? You weren't trying to…"

She covered his mouth with her fingertips, not letting him finish. "Whatever you're about to say, don't. I'm sorry, by the way. I've never shot anyone before."

"No kidding," he said. "What's a girl like you doing with a gun anyway?"

"What do you mean a girl like me?" she asked, frowning.

"A good girl," he said.

"How do you know I'm a good girl?" She wasn't denying it; she was merely curious.

"I just do." He knew because she looked nothing like the women he usually dated. In fact, she was almost the complete opposite of his current girlfriend, Tisha. Tisha had bleach-blond hair with black roots, wore too much makeup, and had a dragon tattooed on her backside. Miss I'm-too-good-for-tattoos Ashleigh wore minimal makeup, had long natural-looking brown hair, and her clothes were conservative, leaving everything to the imagination.

"I like guns," she said.

"You like guns," he repeated, sure she was making it up. There were some women who liked guns, this much he knew. He also knew they looked nothing like her. Though she was young, she resembled the Sunday School teacher he'd had when he was a little kid, the one who had scared him with all her talk of hellfire and brimstone.

"I like guns," she reiterated. "I find solace in target practice and, frankly, I'm a good shot. If you hadn't gotten in my way, I would have kneecapped the guy."

Nick laughed. It hurt, but he did it anyway.

"You don't believe me?" she asked, puffing up like an angry goose.

"Oh, I believe you think you like guns. I believe you think you're a good shot."

She rolled her eyes and sat back. "That's right; you're a marine. Obviously you're a better shot than I am." Her tone was heavy on the sarcasm. He didn't normally bust out his credentials, but this woman was forcing him to make an exception, so he pulled the necklace from around his neck and held it out for her inspection.

"You wear a necklace and that's supposed to convince me you're a better shot than I am," she said.

"Take a closer look," he commanded. She bent and squinted at the necklace, palming it as she turned it over. Her hair brushed his face. It smelled good, like strawberries.

"It's a bullet," she said.

"It's a sniper round."

She tried to hide her reaction and couldn't, especially because she didn't move away from him. When her eyes widened, she was a half an inch from his face. "You're a sniper?" she asked.

He nodded. Her breath was pleasantly minty, and he was temporarily distracted. Up close she was as cute as he'd thought from far away, if you were into the wholesome look, which he wasn't. She was pale, as if she avoided the sun, and the smattering of freckles across her nose told him why. He would bet anything she freckled the minute she stepped into direct sunlight. The freckles were nice, though, as were her eyes, which were sort of a loamy shade of greenish brown. The more he looked at her, the more he liked what he saw, so he stopped paying attention and spoke. "I'm a H.O.G.," he informed her.

"You've lost me."

"A Hunter of Gunmen. It's what we call scout snipers in the corps. Everyone else is a P.I.G., a Professionally Instructed Gunman."

"Why do you wear the necklace?" she was whispering now, either because of awe or because she thought what they were discussing was secret, which it sort of was. He didn't generally go around announcing his career to people who might take exception to it.

"Each person has a round with his name on it. If you're wearing the round, then the bullet can never find you, and you're safe. I never take it off; it's a thing with us."

"Hmm." She tucked the round back in his shirt. He could tell she was trying hard not to be impressed and failing miserably. "How's the gluteus maximus?"

"You can't say butt?" he asked.

She shook her head. "I don't use that word."

He blinked at her, waiting for the punch line, but it never came. "Are you for real?"

"I've never said that word in my life."

"Why not?"

"My dad's a pastor. It went in the list of words we're not allowed to say, along with F-A-R-T and C-R-A-P."

"You're kidding me," he said.

She shook her head.

"Your dad really thinks butt, fart, and crap are curse words?"

"No, they're *coarse* words. There's a difference, but we were taught not to say either one, to keep our language above reproach."

"So, you're like in a cult or something?" he said.

"No, I'm a normal everyday run-of-the-mill Baptist. More conservative than most, probably."

"You think?" he asked. He tried to imagine not cursing and couldn't. Especially since he joined the corps, cursing had become an art form.

"It might surprise you to know I've gotten along fine for twenty two years without ever uttering a curse," she said.

"You're twenty two?" he asked. He wasn't sure if he thought she would be older or younger. She looked younger but acted older.

"Twenty two."

"And you've never said a curse word in your life, not ever," he pressed.

"Not ever."

"What do you say when you smash your finger in the door?"

The doctor pulled back the screen and set out instruments on a tray. Nick tried hard to ignore him and not think about what was about to happen.

"Ouch," Ashleigh replied in answer to his question.

"Okay, what about when you're the most angry you've ever been, really, really frustrated. You have to have some go-to expletive for times like that."

"I do, but it's not a very nice word," she warned.

He smiled. "Lay it on me."

"Blast."

"That's it?" he asked.

"It's not nice; I'm trying to quit."

He stared at her, thinking she was probably a puritan. If he hadn't seen her face down an armed assailant and try to take care of him when he was injured, he might think she had ice water in her veins. Instead he simply thought she was the oddest person he had ever met. "Unbelievable," he said.

"What do you say when you're injured or upset?" she asked.

"I'll give you a hint. It starts with an F."

"Original."

"It's no blast, but it'll do in a pinch."

She laughed and he smiled. When she laughed, she looked like a normal happy twenty-two-year old. A pretty one, too.

"The bullet's wedged deep," the doctor said, interrupting their conversation and dragging Nick back to reality. "The surface is numb, but once I start digging you're going to feel it. Sure you're ready for this?"

"I'm ready," Nick said. Ashleigh offered up her hands, and he held on to them, gripping them tightly in an embarrassing display of nerves. Her hands were stronger than he would have expected and the feel of them in his did something to him, something that felt a whole lot like everything inside him was suddenly melting.

"You can say 'blast' if you want to," she said. "I won't be offended if you steal my word."

Nick laughed and swallowed hard as the doctor began to work.

"What's your name?" Ashleigh whispered.

"Nick," he rasped. Things were really beginning to hurt now, overpowering any attraction he might have felt to her, which was sort of a relief. He didn't need the complication of being attracted to a nun right now. Or ever.

"How much of a distraction do you want me to provide, Nick?" she whispered.

"As much as possible." His eyes squeezed shut on a sickening wave of pain but flew open again in surprise because Ashleigh had leaned forward into the cot, and she was kissing him. His first reaction was to pull back and tell her he wasn't available. But she was offering a distraction, and he was desperate enough to take it. And all of a sudden he very much wanted to be kissing her. So he arched forward and returned her kiss, losing himself in the moment as he forgot the doctor entirely. His only coherent thought was Ashleigh may be a pastor's daughter, but she sure didn't kiss like one.

CHAPTER 3

The metallic plink of the bullet hitting the container startled them out of their kiss. "I think we're done here if you are," the doctor said.

Ashleigh sat back from Nick and bit her chafed lip. "Uh-oh."

They stared at each other as the doctor gave Nick some parting instructions before he and the nurse left, leaving Nick and Ashleigh alone.

"I don't date marines," Ashleigh said. "That was…"

"A distraction," Nick finished for her. "Which is okay because I have a girlfriend."

"Good because I definitely don't date marines who have girl-friends." She should have moved away then, but she didn't. Instead she cupped his face in her hands and leaned in again. Her progress was helped by the fact that Nick did the same to her, reeling her closer. Before they could meet, the screen was ripped aside to reveal three hulking figures who stared at them in surprise.

"Does that treatment come standard at this hospital? If so, will one of you shoot me in the butt?"

"This is Ashleigh. She's a pastor's daughter, and she doesn't say curse words, so keep it clean," Nick warned. "Ashleigh, the chatty one is Kelsey." Their expressions of blunt surprise didn't change as they stared at her.

"You're all marines too, huh?" Ashleigh said.

"What gave it away? Our commanding presence? Our hulking, muscular physiques? Or our 'Ask Me if I'm a Marine' t-shirts?" Kelsey said. Either he was the group spokesperson or none of the others could get in a word.

"Your haircuts. Either you're marines, or there has been a massive lice outbreak wherever you live," Ashleigh said, though in truth it probably was their commanding presence. From a young age, she had always been able to pick out the marines around town. Kelsey was tall and broad shouldered, which automatically made him stand out. The other two men were shorter—one being especially short and young-looking—but she still would have picked them as marines because they had that look, the one that somehow conveyed the fact that when the bullets began to fly they would be the ones running toward them and not away.

Nick had the same look. Even though his right arm was covered with menacing-looking tattoos from shoulder to wrist, he still looked like the guy you would go to whenever you had a problem. It was that indefinable "I've got you covered, you're safe now" air that made those around him feel secure. Maybe that was why she felt drawn to him. Or maybe it was guilt because she had shot him. Or maybe it was those eyes, brown and warm despite the firm set of his mouth that told her he was in a lot more pain than he was copping to. Or maybe it was one of those strange chemical reactions people sometimes have with each other, especially in stressful situations. Whatever the reason, her feelings couldn't be trusted and shouldn't be acted on again.

She wondered if Nick was thinking the same thing because he seemed anxious to get rid of her. "Kelse, Ashleigh's car is stuck at the coffee shop. Why don't you give her a ride and come back for me?"

Ashleigh didn't want to go, but she knew that was the odd chemical reaction part of her talking. The sooner she got away from this man who was so very opposite of her usual type, the better. "That would be great, thanks," Ashleigh said, standing. "You going to make it, marine?"

Nick tilted his head up with a smile. "What do you think?"

I think I'd like to stick around and make sure. Of course she didn't say that, though. She cupped his face again, but this time when she leaned down she bestowed a kiss on his forehead. "I'm sorry about your backside. If there is anything I can do, give me a call. My last name is Desmond and my dad's church is in the book. Call if you need me." Even as she said the words, she knew he wouldn't call.

"Don't worry about it," he said. "I'm glad your weapon of choice is basically a toy. I'd be in real trouble if you favored a Glock."

"I do have a Glock," she said. "It was my birthday present last year."

They shared another smile. He took her hand and pulled it to his lips, kissing her palm. "Get the bleep out of here before I bleeping do something I'll regret," Nick said.

Ashleigh laughed and pulled her hand free.

"Like saying 'bleeping' isn't enough of a regret for you already?" Kelsey said.

Nick glanced at him. "Just get her safely to her car," he said.

"Sir, yes, sir," Kelsey said, and he sounded like he was only half joking that time, making Ashleigh wonder if Nick was some sort of team leader. She followed Kelsey out of the screen without another word, without having met the other two soldiers because it was better that way. Better to get this blip over with and move on.

"So you're a PK," Kelsey said as he held the door for her.

"Guilty. Do you go to church?" Not many people outside the church used the abbreviated PK for preacher's kid.

"A long time ago. What's up with you and Nick?"

"We met this morning and survived an attempted ambush so obviously we're getting married."

He laughed as he held the door of a rickety looking truck, one so tall Ashleigh had to hold on to the door and heft herself up. "You've got a sass mouth for a preacher's kid." He closed the door and leaned in the window. "I like it."

She smiled at him, thinking he was much more her type. He was clean cut with no visible tattoos, and he obviously had at least some knowledge of the church. Not to mention the fact that he was extremely nice looking with his sandy blond hair and piercing, aquamarine eyes. But the strange chemical reaction wasn't there, and that scared her. "How long have you and Nick known each other?"

"Nine years. We met in basic. He probably wouldn't tell you this, but he was such a loser. I basically carried him through." She knew he was teasing her even before he winked. If there was one thing impossible to imagine, it was Nick letting anyone else do the work for him.

"It's amazing you guys ended up here together," she said. Military life was notoriously scattered because a soldier went where the military sent him, no questions.

"It's not amazing," Kelsey said. "It's what we aimed for. We went to, uh, school together for some special training and sort of formed our own team."

"You're a sniper, too?"

Kelsey shot her a look of surprise. "Nick told you?"

She nodded. "I won't tell. I'm not blabby."

"It's not that, it's, well, his current girlfriend doesn't even know what he does. It's not something we talk about because we do so many black ops it makes us and the people we care about targets for some not-so-nice people who would love nothing better than to take out a scout sniper unit." He shook his head. "I can't believe he told you."

Ashleigh couldn't either when he put it like that. "I think we both kind of took each other by surprise today." The truck pulled onto the road and Ashleigh had to reach up to grab the overhead bar to stop herself from bouncing off the seat. "How are you planning to get Nick home today?"

Kelsey thumbed the bed of the truck over his shoulder.

"You're kidding, right?" Ashleigh asked.

"Usually, but no. He can lie down back there. I brought a sleeping bag." He pointed to a rolled up bag at his feet.

"No," Ashleigh said.

"What do you mean no?" Kelsey asked. He glanced at her from his peripheral vision.

"Just no. You can't put a man who was shot in the backside in this thing, and especially not back there. That would be excruciatingly painful for him."

"It's like five minutes to home. He'll be fine."

"No," Ashleigh said. "Not happening."

"Uh, excuse me, PK, but what does this have to do with you? You can't tell us how Nick is or isn't getting home," Kelsey said. Ashleigh had the impression he didn't get angry very often, but he was definitely getting there now. "And there is nothing wrong with my truck," he added.

She didn't care, though, because she knew she was right on this one. "This has everything to do with me because I'm the one who shot him."

That shut him up. "I thought the guy he took down shot him."

"Nope. It was me and, as such, that makes him my responsibility. It was bad enough watching him get the bullet dug out with basically an aspirin as pain reliever. I'm not going to have him riding home in this bucket of rust. He can ride in my perfectly nice and boring sedan where he can lie down in the back seat. It has these new things called shock absorbers. You should give them a try."

Kelsey rubbed his hands over the steering wheel a couple of times, thinking. "I'm not sure I like you," he said at last. "Which is odd because I always like Nick's girlfriends."

"I'm not his girlfriend, and I have no plans to be. And, for the record, people usually don't like me at first. I'm abrasive, and I know it, but I see things the way they should be, and I try to make them that way to the exclusion of everything around me, sometimes including people's feelings. I'm not going to apologize for doing what is right, ever, and driving Nick in my car is the right thing to do. I'll take him home, deposit him safely in his bed, and then I'll be out of your life forever."

"Has anyone ever told you you remind them of a drill instructor?" Kelsey asked.

"Yes, actually, but then he asked me to marry him, so I'm not really sure what that means."

Kelsey managed a smile, looking relieved. "So you're engaged."

She shook her head, turning to look out the window. "Didn't work out." They arrived at Starbucks and she pointed to her car. "That one. I'll see you back at the hospital in a few."

"Sir, yes, sir," Kelsey muttered as Ashleigh hopped down from the truck and darted away.

CHAPTER 4

*N*ick didn't look happy to see her.

"What's she doing here?" he asked Kelsey.

"She followed me home. Can we keep her?" Kelsey said.

"I'm giving you a ride home," Ashleigh explained. "I saw the rusty bucket and figured I would save you the lockjaw you would surely receive if you rode in there, to say nothing of the pain of bumping around."

"Did she make fun of my truck? Did you hear that?" Kelsey looked at the two other marines who still hadn't said a word as far as Ashleigh could tell.

"'Truck,'" Ashleigh said, holding up her hands to make air quotes. "That's generous. Rust and rubber with an axle is more apt, am I right?" She turned to Tweedledee and Tweedledum, but they remained wisely silent, though one of them was smiling, the short one who looked Latino.

"What the crud, Lolly? You're taking her side?" Kelsey asked, and the little marine lost his smile, shaking his head.

"Let's get out of here," Nick said. His tone was longsuffering and she wondered what he was really feeling. He seemed to use exasperation as a cover for lots of other things, though exasperation was better than rage any day. From the waist down, he was covered by a thin piece of paper, something that was supposed to be a blanket but wouldn't pass for one in the real world. On top, he was wearing a hospital gown.

"Here, I keep extra clothes in my car. I brought this for you." She handed him a skirt. It was long, and it had an elastic waistband. Even so, it would probably still be tight, but it was better than nothing.

"A skirt," he said, unfurling it. "No way." He wadded it up and attempted to hand it back to her.

"Okay. Naked works, too. Get off the gurney, and I'll keep my eyes closed as I lead you to my car." She crossed her arms over her chest and stared him down.

He glanced at his friends. "You couldn't have brought me underwear and pants?"

"And miss the show?" Kelsey said. "Hey, PK, do you have a bra for him? I'm pretty sure I read somewhere bras are good for butt injuries, plus it'll match the skirt."

"Could you for once in our lives shut it?" Nick made a closing motion with his hand.

"No," Kelsey replied.

"I didn't think so, but it was worth a shot," Nick said. He closed his eyes as he rolled off the gurney, fighting a wave of nausea and dizziness when he was finally on his feet. Then his eyes flew open in surprise because Ashleigh was there, supporting him with her arm around his waist.

"You're looking a little green, marine," she said, smiling in a tender sort of way that tugged at his heart. It wasn't a romantic moment, more like the way a mother might smile at her little boy, but it still made his heart ache because he hadn't been the recipient of that sort of look in a long time. Maybe ever.

"It's the camo paint," Kelsey said. "Eventually it soaks into the skin and makes us all green. You think Kermit is a frog? No. He spent too many years in the corps. Biggest secret in Hollywood."

"He doesn't have an off switch, does he?" Ashleigh asked.

"None that I've been able to find, but that doesn't stop me from looking," Nick said. She unfurled the skirt and held it out at his feet. The flimsy gown covered him in front, but still, she was a little too close for comfort.

"What are the odds of you backing off to let me do this myself?" he asked.

"About as good as hoping Kelsey will magically stop talking," she said.

"Hey," Kelsey said. "I can shut up any time I want. All you have to do is ask. You say the word, and I'm quiet. Mute. Totally silent. Not a peep. No sounds. Words equal gone. Lips not moving. Helen Keller of the marine world…" He would have kept going, but one of the truly silent marines jabbed him in the shoulder and he actually stopped talking.

Nick lifted one foot. He only got it three inches off the ground, but Ashleigh shimmied the skirt underneath and stretched it, waiting for him to lift the other foot. He would never admit it, but he was glad for the help. Without her, he would have been forced to lift his leg to regular height, tearing his stitches, to say nothing of the pain. As it was, he was sweating. Theoretically he knew how many bodily movements the butt controlled, but experiencing it was another matter entirely. It almost hurt to smile, not that he had much to smile about at the moment.

He lifted his other leg and Ashleigh got the skirt on. She began pulling it up, shimmying the fabric because, even though it was elastic, he was much larger than she and it was stretched tight. She reached his waist and carefully kept her hands at his sides, skimming her hands over his hip bones when the skirt stuck. Then she cautiously reached behind and pulled the elastic out so it wouldn't scrape his wound. Even though she was being careful, it still hurt. And it was an intensely intimate moment as he stood there, helpless as a toddler while she ran her hands over his body from an inch away. He was thankful for the pain because it distracted him from the reality of her closeness and the pleasure of her touch. Had anyone's hands ever been so soft and gentle on him? He didn't think so.

He wondered if she was as affected as he was as she finished and took a step back. "There," she whispered. "All set." They stared at each other, heat and chemistry bouncing palpably between them.

"Weirdest moment of my life," Kelsey declared. "And that's saying something. You ready Nicole?" he asked, eyeing Nick's new outfit with a curled lip. "It's going to take a lot of blows to the head to make me forget this image."

"Want me to help you get started?" Ashleigh asked. The little marine laughed, and everyone turned to him in surprise.

"What? She's funny," he said. He had the barest trace of a Spanish accent and kind eyes. He and Ashleigh shared a smile and she knew at least one of Nick's friends liked her. Not that it mattered because after she did her duty and dropped him off, she was removing herself from temptation. A ride to his house, and that was all.

Ashleigh was ready to offer her support, but Kelsey stepped forward and put his arm around Nick, taking much more of his weight than she would have been able to. "Come on, sweetheart. Let's get you home before your five o'clock shadow appears and people realize you're actually a man," he said.

Ashleigh couldn't help it; she laughed.

Nick turned to look at her. "Traitor. You're not supposed to humor him." He reached out his free arm and rested it companionably on her shoulders, pulling her closer. She slipped her arm around his waist to add her own support, but with Kelsey holding up his other side she was more decorative than actually helpful.

"Oh, good, add her to the train because now we look much more normal," Kelsey said. "Just a cross-dressing marine, his best friend, and his whatever the new girl is out for a stroll. No biggie. Stop staring," he muttered.

Ashleigh snickered and Nick squeezed her shoulders. She looked up at him and her smile died because he was pale and sweating. Suddenly she felt horrible because, without a doubt, this was all her fault. The guy with the gun at Starbucks had lowered his weapon on her, and she had responded. She hadn't even seen Nick because it was as if he materialized from nowhere. If she had noticed him, if she had thought he was going to tackle the guy, then of course she wouldn't have shot. But everything happened so fast she had thought the blurry movement was the guy shooting someone. So she had shot, and now Nick was in horrible pain.

Tears blurred her vision, and she blinked them away. If there was one thing marines feared, it was a crying woman. Now wasn't the time. Maybe she would cry later when she was alone. For now she concentrated on getting Nick safely to her car.

They reached it and she held the door while Kelsey deposited Nick onto his stomach with a "See you at home, princess." He left and she knelt so she could see Nick's face.

"Okay?" she asked.

"I'm fine," he said, which he would undoubtedly say even if one of his legs and arms suddenly fell off.

She brushed her hand over his forehead, mimicking the motion of smoothing his hair from his eyes if his hair had been longer than a half inch all over his head. "I'm really sorry about this."

"It's okay," Nick said. "I mean, it's not, but it is because I know your intentions were good. And, hey, if I hadn't been there, you would have been a hero for kneecapping the guy. So try not to beat yourself up, okay? You were doing what you thought you had to do."

She wondered if that was what he told himself as he went on missions because basically he was a hired gun. The government told him where to point the gun and when to pull the trigger, but in essence he was a hired killer. She wanted to ask him about it, ask him if it bothered him, but something told her he got that question a lot and it annoyed him. And there was the fact that she was trying to keep her distance. A ride home, and that was it. Ten minutes of driving, and she would be out of his life forever.

So she left him, closing the door on his sweaty, upturned face as she slid behind the wheel. She should have felt relieved over the fact that her disconcerting reaction to this man was almost at an end, but she didn't. In fact, she felt the opposite of relieved. As she followed Kelsey's rattletrap truck through the streets of Camp LeJeune, she felt not merely sad, but empty somehow, as if she were losing something vital, which was crazy. She had just met the man. All she knew about him was he was a marine, and she wasn't the type of woman to go gaga over a man merely because he carried a gun and wore a uniform, at least not anymore. What was it then? What was it about this man that made her feel like when she walked away she would be leaving a piece of herself behind?

When they pulled into his driveway, she still didn't have an answer to that question, and now it was time to go.

CHAPTER 5

"This house is huge," Ashleigh commented.

"We each like to have our own bedroom," Nick said. His voice was muffled because his face was pressed to the seat as he waited for Kelsey to retrieve him. "We split the rent, of course, so it ends up being cheaper than living on base. And, I don't know, it feels a little more like home this way, you know?"

"I'm not carrying you over the threshold," Kelsey said as he leaned in the car and pulled Nick out.

"You did that when we moved in, so I think we're covered," Nick said.

Kelsey laughed and Ashleigh smiled. They were obviously close. She was both glad for them and a little envious because she had never been that close to another person besides her parents. She followed behind while they made slow progress to the house. She had intended to see Nick to his room and leave, but as soon as they walked inside she stopped short and looked around. It looked and smelled exactly like a locker room. Clothes were strewn everywhere. There were a couple of mismatched, worn-looking couches with a huge television and state of the art game system. Empty cans and food containers littered the coffee table and floor. It wasn't a sty, but it was close.

"We, uh, weren't expecting any guests today," Nick said, his tone sheepish as he took in her inspection.

"You want to go to your room or to the couch?" Kelsey asked.

"The couch," Nick said. His answer had been so quick Ashley suspected his room was even messier than the rest of the house.

"Let me get you a glass of water," Ashleigh said. Nick protested, but she ignored him and picked her way to the kitchen, stepping over piles of trash. The kitchen was exactly as she suspected: empty of everything but dirty dishes and more trash. A quick peek in the refrigerator revealed a bottle of ketchup, a case of beer, and three partially consumed bottles of wine. She walked back out of the kitchen, sans water, and sat on the couch beside Nick's head.

"Yeah, I'm not leaving you like this," she declared.

"What do you mean?" he asked. "I'm fine."

"You're not fine. There's no food in the kitchen." She didn't mention the trash, not wanting to offend him over something that was none of her business. His wellbeing was her business, however.

"We'll get takeout. We always do."

Ashleigh blinked at him as if not understanding the words. "You can't eat takeout when you're sick. You need good food and lots of TLC. Are your sheets clean? Because you can't lie on dirty sheets with that wound. You could get an infection."

"I, uh, sort of don't have sheets on the bed. There were some, but I lost them somehow."

"I think Lolly took them after he bled through his," Kelsey said. He was on the recliner watching a game and obviously eavesdropping.

"Okay, that settles it. I'm staying here until I feel comfortable enough to leave you. I'm going to get you some sheets, and I'm going to cook you something wholesome."

"Ashleigh, you don't have to do that. I'm fine here. I know this place looks bad, but it's home. I'm used to it. Please go." He probably sounded a little desperate, but that was okay because he felt desperate. He had to get away from her, to get some space so he could get her out of his system. No way was he throwing away Tisha and his happy life for the church lady.

"I shot you. Doesn't that entitle me to perform a little indentured servitude on your behalf?" she asked.

"If so, then we would be cleaning somebody's house in Afghanistan right now," Kelsey said, not taking his eyes off the television.

"Please," Ashleigh added. "This would go a long way toward assuaging my guilt."

"The woman wants to cook and clean for you, I say let her," Kelsey said. "Never look a gift maid in the mouth."

Ashleigh looked around for an empty can—which wasn't hard to find—and tossed it at his head, pinging it off his temple. "Nice aim," he said, still not bothering to turn and look at her.

"I don't know that it's a good idea," Nick said, but he was wavering. For better or worse, he wanted her to stay. The rational part of him knew it was good for her to leave, but the emotional part, the part that liked it when she brushed her hand over his forehead, definitely wanted her to stay. She brushed her hand over his face again, this time smoothing down the side and resting her palm on his cheek.

"Please," she said. "I owe you one."

"Okay," he agreed. They got caught up looking at each other a few beats until the front door slammed and someone entered.

"Hey, Melly, let yourself in and make yourself at home," Kelsey said, though how he knew it was Melly was beyond Ashleigh because he was still staring at ESPN as if it held the answers to life's biggest questions.

The woman, Melly, frowned at the back of his head. She was petite and curvaceous with long dark hair and an equally dark complexion. She had the sort of over the top exotic beauty Ashleigh had always envied, like Tropical Barbie. "If you idiots didn't want me to let myself in, you shouldn't have given me a key," she said.

"The key was for when we're not here," Kelsey said.

"You didn't specify," she argued.

"What if I had a woman in here?" Kelsey asked.

"Then I would warn her to run as far and as fast as possible. Where's my baby brother?"

"Lolly? We chopped him up and buried him in the back yard. Or he's in his room like he is every time you ask that question," Kelsey replied.

Melly made a face, but it was lost on the back of his head. She glanced at Ashleigh, still frowning. "Who's she?"

"She's Nick's new girl," Kelsey answered.

"What happened to Tisha?"

"Good question, one I'm sure Tisha will want an answer to when she shows up next. Should be a good catfight. Advance tickets are half price, but you'll pay double at the door. See me later with your money," Kelsey said.

Melly muttered something in Spanish and walked away.

"Don't forget my laundry," Kelsey called. "Use that oxy stuff on the whites. It's good for getting out odors."

In answer, a door halfway down the hall slammed, rattling its hinges.

"Woman loves me," Kelsey said.

Ashleigh gave Nick a questioning glance. "They have a whole love/hate thing going. It's really fun for the rest of us who have to listen to their incessant bickering."

"What size is your bed?" Ashleigh asked.

"King," Nick said. His eyes closed because she was once again soothing her fingers over his head, this time through his hair, and it felt so good.

"If I'm going to cook, I'm going to need to clean the kitchen. Is that okay?" she asked.

"Clean away," Nick mumbled. He hadn't felt this sleepy in ages. Ashleigh stood and somehow located a blanket. When she covered him, it was the last thing he remembered.

"Which one is Nick's room?" she asked Kelsey.

"Third door on the right. Make sure and precision fold his shirts. He's picky about that."

She took two steps, stopped, and turned back to him. "Which one is his room really?"

"That was so close to working," Kelsey said. "Second door on the right."

She eased down the hall and peeked into the room, feeling like an intruder. Not that he would notice her presence, however. The place was a wreck. There were no sheets on the bed, and what blanket there was lay haphazardly dragging the floor. She was tempted to buy a comforter, something pretty that would liven up the drab khaki walls, but that would be so far over the line she probably wouldn't be able to see the line anymore. She wasn't his girlfriend or his decorator; she was his…what was she? Woman who was making restitution. There. Certainly a set of sheets could be seen as restitution, couldn't they?

His clothes were everywhere. At first she picked them up and began sniffing before realizing they were all dirty and needed washed. The only thing in his closet was his dress uniform, and she knew that had to be dry clean only, so she didn't touch it. She did, however, pause to admire it. Marines certainly knew how to look good when they wanted to.

She sorted the clothes on the bed and went to find Kelsey for another question. "Do you guys have a washing machine?"

He finally tore his attention off the television to blink at her in confusion. "What is this washing machine you speak of?"

"I'll take that as a no, then." She sighed, hating the thought of going to the Laundromat when it was already going to take her forever to clean the kitchen and make supper. But then Melly exited the third room on the right, Kelsey's room

"Your laundry is done, Jaws," she said. Her tone was full of amusement and self-satisfaction, and Ashleigh wasn't the only one who noticed because Kelsey stood up, towering over both women.

"What did you do, Melly?"

"I took care of the stink for you as requested, sir," she said, trying and failing to look humble. She tried to sidestep him and head for the door, but he picked her up around the waist and carried her down the hall to his room while she squealed and tried to get away.

They were only in the room for a second before they ran back out again, their hands over their noses. "I cannot believe you set off a stink bomb in my hamper," Kelsey said. He bent over, gagging. "What are you, twelve?"

"Me?" Melly said, pointing to her chest. "You want to talk about how you showed up near the end of my last date and begged me to come home to our children? I liked that guy."

"That guy was a loser and a jerk and you wouldn't listen to me. What was I supposed to do?"

"Not pretending to cry on his shoulder over baby Johnny's impetigo would have been a good start," Melly said. She pointed down the hall toward his room. "You had that coming and then some. You've had it coming since I met you." She stormed to the entrance and paused with her hand on the door. "Here's a little tip for you, Jaws. Try the oxy stuff. I hear it works wonders for odors." After delivering her parting shot, she jerked open the door and walked outside, slamming it behind her.

Ashleigh glanced at Nick, but he had slept through the whole encounter. She wondered if that meant the same sort of thing happened often.

"Hey, PK," Kelsey began, "you're going to do Nick's laundry, right? Could you maybe…" he let the thought hang.

"No way. I am not touching your stink bomb laundry. In fact, why don't you take Nick's clothes?"

"I don't think you want his in the same vicinity as mine. It's bad. I might have to throw these away and get new." He scowled at the door and Ashleigh knew he was imagining Melly in place of the door.

"Let's compromise," Ashleigh said. "I'll take the clothes and get them started. You can go change them over and wait for them to dry while I clean the kitchen and make supper."

He gave a longsuffering sigh. "All right, but the kitchen better be really clean and the supper really good."

"I'll do my best," she said. He went to stuff his clothes into heavy-duty trash bags to try and contain the smell while she located a few laundry baskets for Nick's clothes. The fact that he had laundry baskets gave her hope he at least tried to be organized sometimes.

They loaded her car together and she drove to the nearest laundry place, conveniently located a few blocks away. After loading all their clothes in the machines, she went to the store and bought food along with a set of sheets for Nick.

When she arrived back at the house, Nick was still asleep. Ashleigh unloaded her groceries into the fridge and set to work on cleaning up. To her relief, it wasn't as bad as it looked. They had a dishwasher, so she loaded everything that would fit, threw away all the trash, scrubbed the counters, sinks, and floor, and she was done, at least with the cleaning portion of things. The food would take a while, but she had time.

She had chosen to make her family's specialty of chicken pot pie. It was time consuming because she made the broth from scratch, but if she hurried she could get the whole thing done in an hour and a half, especially because she had started the broth as soon as she arrived and it was now finished. She added potatoes, carrots, and celery. While those cooked, she assembled a peach cobbler for dessert and set it in the oven to bake. Turning her attention back to the pot pie, she made a roux and combined everything, pouring the concoction into the premade crusts she had purchased at the store. Buying crust instead of making it from scratch was cheating and enough to shame her family honor, but there was only so much she could do in a day.

Because it was North Carolina, she also made sweet tea and then everything was ready, including the dishes which were ready to be emptied from the dishwasher, in time to set the table. As she finished setting the table, she turned to call the men to dinner, but there was no need. They were there.

"It smells edible in here. What have you done, devil woman?" This came from Kelsey, of course, who sat and flicked open his napkin, resting it in his lap.

"Did you finish your laundry?" she asked.

"Yes, Ma, and I washed my hands." He held out his nails for her inspection. She flicked his knuckle as she passed by.

"I asked because I was wondering if you were able to get the smell out," she explained.

"Mostly. I'm afraid when I sweat it's all going to come back, though. Your sister is insane." He said the last part to the guy they called Lolly as he sat.

"Whoo, she was steamed at you, Bro. Should have heard her bust out the Spanish in my room," Lolly replied.

"Yeah, well, she's gonna get it for this one. Nobody stink bombs my Underoos and gets away with it."

"There's so much wrong with that sentence I don't know where to start," Nick said. He had been standing silently to the side, observing Ashleigh as she buzzed around setting dishes on the table. She paused beside him.

"I grabbed your donut from the hospital after you accidentally forgot it," she said. "It's on your chair." She pointed to the table, and he grimaced.

"You don't really expect me to sit on that thing, do you?" he asked.

"What do you think?" she quirked an eyebrow and pinned him with a stare he was beginning to recognize. He would never tell her as much, but he was frightened by that look. Somehow it held as much determination as anyone he had ever encountered in the corps. There would be no winning an argument with the woman once her mind was made up. Thankfully his protest was only half-hearted because he was secretly relieved she had insisted on bringing the rubber donut from the hospital. His behind was killing him.

"Fine, but only because you're cute," he said. She laughed and pulled out his chair, resting her hand on his back as she assisted him to the table.

"Oh, you're good, Marine."

There was a lot he could have said in response to that statement, most of it inappropriate, so he refrained. He wondered if she would even understand his innuendo if he used it on her. How innocent was she? Had she dated a man? Obviously she knew how to kiss, but was she one of those who drew the line there? He couldn't imagine a twenty-two year old virgin, but then he couldn't have imagined someone like Ashleigh before he met her. She wasn't like any of the women he had encountered before. He hadn't been kidding when he said she was a good girl. Women like her didn't mix with men like him. They should have been like oil and water. Why, then, was there that strange flicker of attraction between them?

"I'm Ashleigh," she said as she poured a glass of tea for Truck.

"I'm Truck," he replied. Truck usually drank a beer with supper. He looked to Nick for direction, and Nick shook his head. Truck rolled his eyes, but Ashleigh wasn't looking, so Nick didn't call him on it.

At last she sat. The four marines reached simultaneously toward the center of the table before realizing her eyes were closed. Would she make them pray? But, no, she seemed to be doing that on her own. They froze nonetheless, which would have been hilarious to any of their other teammates. They were trained to be unfazed, to let nothing and no one stop them from accomplishing their goal, and yet the sight of a woman praying had immobilized them.

Ashleigh opened her eyes and smiled as if she saw nothing amiss with four men having their arms dangling over the table in midair. "May I serve you?" she asked, standing.

They withdrew their hands because what man in his right mind would say no to June Cleaver when she was offering to dish up the delicious meal she had spent all afternoon cooking?

"I suppose," Kelsey said, adding in a heavy sigh as if it pained him to have a woman offer him a plate of steaming pie. Nick glanced at Ashleigh to see if she understood Kelsey's sense of humor yet, and her smile looked unchanged. He took that as a good sign.

"So, y'all have nicknames," Ashleigh said when she finished serving them and sat down.

"Did she y'all us?" Kelsey asked.

"Welcome to North Carolina," she said.

"We have nicknames," Nick said. "Truck's real name is Ashton." Kelsey snickered until Ashton reached over and clapped him on the back of the head.

"Something funny *Kelsey*?" he asked. He had a trace of a southern accent, not too different than Ashleigh's. She wondered where he was from, but he didn't seem open to questions.

Kelsey shook his head and cleared his throat, concentrating on his food.

"I heard Melly call you Jaws," Ashleigh said to the top of his head. "What's that about?"

"It's short for Jabber Jaws," Truck said. "On account of he never shuts up."

Kelsey opened his mouth and showed Truck his masticated food. Ashleigh thought it unbelievable these men who acted like teenage boys were somehow responsible for the safety of the country.

"Lolly," she said, turning her attention to the baby-faced man to her left. "What's that for?"

"It's because he represents the Lollypop Guild," Kelsey answered. "You know--a munchkin."

"Aw," Ashleigh said. She knew the little marine wouldn't want her pity, but she couldn't help it. He was so cute and sweet looking, like a puppy who wanted attention.

"Don't let that face fool you, Ash. Lolly's our point man," Nick said.

"I've heard that term, but I don't know exactly what it means," Ashleigh said.

"He's the guy who walks in front, scouting the area for hostiles or IED's," Truck answered.

Ashleigh inspected Lolly again. His head was down now as if he were uncomfortable being the topic of conversation. This guy who looked even younger than her was the one who walked ahead of everyone else? Unbelievable.

"What do you do?" she asked Truck.

"I drive the truck," he said.

The other guys laughed and Lolly finally looked up. "He's the machine gunner. He brings up the rear and shoots anyone who tries to come at us from behind. After everyone has been blown to smithereens, *then* he drives the truck." He smiled, a sweet angelic smile in contrast to his seemingly gleeful tone at the thought of Truck blowing people to smithereens. She pulled her gaze from him and addressed Nick.

"And you and Kelsey are both the shooters?" She prided herself on not stumbling over the word "shooters."

"Yes and no," Nick replied. "We're both trained to do the same thing, but Kelsey is the spotter and I'm the shooter. We can switch it up in a pinch, but it's better if we stay in our preserved roles."

"The spotter. You've lost me again."

"I literally spot the target and watch the vapor trail to track the trajectory of the bullet," Kelsey explained.

"You can see a bullet's vapor trail?" Ashleigh asked.

"I can. You can't. It takes training and practice."

"And he's armed with an automatic rifle," Nick said. "My weapon is not something that's used up close or quickly. If someone gets the drop on us, it's up to him to take them out. Kelsey is literally watching my back when we're on assignment."

"Oh," Ashleigh said. She didn't want to appear like she was in awe of them, even though she was. Their jobs were not only highly dangerous, but they were highly skilled, too. Previously she had thought all that went into being a sniper was pointing and shooting, but it took a whole team to make things work. "My job doesn't seem awesome at all anymore," she added because they seemed to be waiting for her to say something.

"What is your job?" Nick asked. "Shouldn't you be in college?"

"I skipped college and went to trade school. I'm a carpenter."

She had surprised them, but she was used to that. No one seemed able to believe a woman was capable of being a carpenter. Finally Kelsey spoke.

"Did you choose that because Jesus was a carpenter? Because that seems like taking things to the extreme."

"Yes. I'm also planning to die at thirty three and change some water into wine." She wadded her napkin and tossed it at him. "No. I chose it because when I was little my parents bought this behemoth fixer upper and they could never get anyone to do any work on it. My dad always used to say if someone was a skilled worker and had good business sense he, or she, could make a million dollars. I decided to see if that was true. At first people are suspicious of me because I'm a woman, but then they realize I actually show up when I say I'll show up and complete the job by the scheduled time, and they're convinced."

"I'm not convinced," Kelsey said. "Go build a window seat in my room, and if it meets my exacting standards, *then* I'll consider giving you my approval."

"Can I serve dessert first?" Ashleigh asked.

Kelsey rolled his eyes. "Geez, high maintenance much? Fine. Serve dessert."

"A carpenter," Nick said. "That's so awesome."

"Hey, what's your nickname?" she asked.

"It's Whit," Kelsey supplied. "Short for Whitman."

"I don't get it," she said.

"The poet. You know, 'O Captain, My Captain.' Nick is our fearless leader," Kelsey said.

"Are you a captain?" Ashleigh asked.

Nick shook his head, looking uncomfortable. "Nah, I'm not even an officer. I'm a corporal."

Kelsey spoke by pretending to cough into his hand. "Waste of talent."

"Kelse," Nick warned.

"What are you gonna do, donut boy? Beat me with your cushy rubberized tube?"

"No, I'm going to remember this moment for when I'm back on my feet again," Nick said, and Kelsey shut up.

"Dessert," Ashleigh announced, glad for a reprieve from the awkwardness. She returned with warm peach cobbler and set it on the table, noting as she did so the chicken pot pie was all gone, even though she had doubled the amount she usually made. Nick grabbed her hand and held it before she could cut into the cobbler.

"Thanks for this. It was amazing. Everything has been amazing. I really appreciate it."

"You're welcome," Ashleigh said. They were stuck again, staring at each other, but not for long because the door opened and closed and a voice rang out, calling Nick's name.

Kelsey sat back with a smile. "Looks like Tisha's here." He made a pawing motion in the air. "Meow."

CHAPTER 6

"Who's she?" Tisha walked in and stopped short, staring at Ashleigh. Kelsey's comment about a cat fight made sense because Tisha looked very much like a feline who was staking out her territory. Her back was definitely up. But Ashleigh wasn't there to try and stake her own territory because this wasn't her territory. She was doing a good deed, and then she was going home.

"I'm Ashleigh," she said. "The pot pie is gone, but can I get you some cobbler?"

Tisha blinked at her as if she hadn't understood any of the words. She glanced at Nick, searching for an explanation. "You guys hire a cook?"

"No, um, Ashleigh and I met today and she sort of volunteered to cook for me. It's a long story," Nick said. Ashleigh knew, even if he didn't, that his explanation had the opposite effect of soothing Tisha, so she jumped in and tried to help him.

"I'm the one who accidentally shot him this morning. I'm trying to make amends a little and help out." Right away she realized her mistake because Tisha turned stricken eyes to Nick.

"What the…You were shot and you didn't tell me?"

"Tish, it was no big deal. I didn't want to bother you at work."

"Bother me? You think calling to tell me you got shot counts as bothering me?"

She was gearing up to explode, and Ashleigh definitely didn't want to be there when that happened. She dished up the cobbler, bypassing her own portion by giving it to Tisha, and then set down the spoon.

"I should probably get home." She wanted to tell Nick to call her if he needed anything, but she knew he wouldn't and it wasn't the type of thing to say in front of his angry girlfriend. "Take care," she said instead, hoping her eyes didn't betray all she was feeling.

"Let me walk you out," Nick said, and she winced. Tisha was definitely not going to like that.

"I'll do it," Lolly said. He stood and set his napkin on the table before Nick could try and get to his feet.

"Thank you," Ashleigh said, grateful he was saving her from any further awkwardness. He smiled as he stepped back to let her pass and held the door for her when they reached it.

"It was really nice to meet you, Ashleigh. I hope we'll see more of you. I think you'd be really good for Nick," he said as soon as they were safely on the porch.

"I really enjoyed meeting you today, too, but I don't foresee a future for Nick and myself. He has a girlfriend, and I…" She was going to say she wasn't interested, but that wasn't quite true anymore. "Well, I don't think it would work. We're very different."

Lolly glanced at the house as if deciding whether or not to say what he obviously wanted to say. "Nick is a great guy, and if he could learn to get rid of those inner demons, then he would be an awesome guy. He doesn't see it, but he could go all the way in the marines. Someone like you could help him with that."

"I can't fix anyone," Ashleigh said. She knew because she had tried once before and failed miserably.

"No, but you know Someone who can."

Was he really telling her Nick needed to find God? "Are you Baptist?" she asked.

He laughed. "Dios, no, don't even joke or my mamma will turn over in her grave. I'm Catholic. The guys give me a hard time for being devout. Maybe I'm fooling myself, but I think they're a little envious. But we go out on these missions and they look to me, the littlest, youngest guy for the answers to life's biggest questions, you know? We've spent a lot of time talking, more than most people spend together in a lifetime, and I can tell you they're all searching for something, Nick most of all."

Ashleigh took a breath, held it, and let it out slowly. "There was a time when I was young and optimistic. I would have seen Nick as a challenge, and I would have tried to help him, to lead him to some answers. But I've been down that road, and it didn't work. I don't think I have it in me to try again."

"Someone hurt you," Lolly guessed.

She nodded.

"Physically?"

She nodded again.

"Was he a marine?"

"Yes," Ashleigh replied.

Lolly turned his head to the side and spat. "He's not a marine, not in spirit, anyway. We would never hurt a woman, and Nick especially would never do such a thing. If he would, then I wouldn't put my complete faith in him as I have. Don't judge all men or all marines by that one bad example." He clenched and unclenched his fists. "Is he still stationed here?"

She shook her head. "He's in Quantico."

"He's training to be an officer?" Lolly guessed.

She nodded.

"Sometimes the world is a mixed up place. But you have my word, Ashleigh, if this man ever comes back and bothers you again, then we'll protect you. Even if it means we have to kill him."

Ashleigh wasn't sure how to feel about that statement, mostly because she knew he was serious. While other people might flippantly toss around the phrase "I'll kill him," she knew this man meant it. "I don't want that, but thank you."

"You may not want it, but sometimes when evil is so great, death is the only solution."

"He's not evil. He's a very messed up man," she said.

"What's the difference?" Lolly asked. His eyes had changed from soft to hard, and Ashleigh repressed a shudder. Perhaps war had done its own sort of damage to Lolly.

She rested her hand on his bicep and gave it a squeeze. "You okay?"

He forced a smile and pulled his gaze back from wherever it had gone. "I'm good. Sometimes things are hard, but I'm lucky. I have a soft place to fall."

"Your sister?" she guessed.

"Yes. Melly doesn't ever let me hold my emotions inside where they can eat away at me. She's my own form of therapy, forcing me to deal with my issues whenever they arise. I'm the only one with a family connection like that. The other guys, I worry." He turned to look at the house with a frown.

"You know, that offer goes both ways, Lolly. If you ever need anything, a friend, a listening ear, someone to go to the movies with when you want to blow off some steam, I'm here."

"Thanks, Ashleigh." They looked each other over for a few beats. It was strange how different it was from the way she and Nick looked at each other. She and Lolly had their own sort of chemistry, but it wasn't romantic; it was more an instantaneous bond of friendship and mutual understanding.

"What's your real name?" she asked.

"I don't want to tell you. You'll laugh," he said.

"Try me," she prompted.

"Jesus."

She didn't laugh, but she did have to bite her lip. "That must be a difficult name for a marine to carry around."

"You have no idea," he said. "I was ecstatic when they started calling me Lolly."

They shared another smile, then he held her door and stood in the driveway, watching until she drove away.

CHAPTER 7

The next morning, Nick woke up on sheets that somehow smelled like Ashleigh, even though they were new. Her scent must have rubbed off on them as she was putting them on his bed. Or maybe her smell was permanently stuck in his nose as a way to torment. Not that it was a bad smell; it was a delicious smell, a mix of coconut, lime, and vanilla. But it was tormenting because it was a reminder of what was so far out of reach.

Last night had been a blip, but an interesting one nonetheless. Tisha did the best she could for him, always trying to be there to meet his needs whenever they arose. The problem was she was as messed up as he was, so she had very little to offer. She was so busy trying to work on her own issues she didn't often have mental or emotional energy to work on his. Last night had been a fascinating glimpse into what life was like with a woman like Ashleigh. Someone who cooked dinner, did laundry, and cleaned up. Someone who thought sheets on the bed were a necessity and not a luxury. Tisha didn't have sheets on her bed, either.

His thoughts were scattered and borderline melancholy, and he didn't like that. He wasn't a mopey person. He was a man of action, which was why it was all the more frustrating he was down for the count for the next week. What did he have to do but lie around and think of Ashleigh and what might have been if life were a little bit different? If he had been born to a good family who actually cared about him and taught him how to be a decent human being, then maybe he would be the man for Ashleigh. They could be average together with a nice little vanilla family, mortgage, and boring sedan. Maybe he would coach his kid's soccer team on the weekend. Instead he rented a house with three other guys who were as clueless about life as he was. Well, maybe Lolly had things figured out, but he was too young and too shy to do anything about it.

Would he be forty and still acting like a teenager, hopping from girlfriend to girlfriend, never having more than a hundred dollars in the bank at any given time, always looking for the next party to take his mind off the misery of his life? He didn't want that, but he had no idea how to change it. The corps had given him a roadmap for his life, at least when it came to his career. They taught him how to have honor, discipline, and courage. He loved his job. He only wished he knew how to apply those lessons on the outside because when it came to real life he was clueless.

His phone rang, and he was glad for the distraction from his dreary thoughts. "Hello."

"Corporal Lassiter, this is Sergeant Hart of the Jacksonville Police Department. You met one of my officers yesterday at Starbucks."

"Yes, sir, go ahead."

"I'm interviewing the woman who shot you this morning, and I wanted to check with you and make sure you don't want to press charges."

Nick sat up and winced before remembering his injury and falling back on his bed again. "What? Why are you interviewing Ashleigh? Why would I want to press charges?"

"It's standard procedure whenever a shot is fired, especially in a place of business. We need to go over her version of events and make sure no laws were broken."

"They weren't," Nick insisted. "She was trying to protect those people. If I hadn't been there, it would have been her against the gunman. She might have died for what she did. She should be given a commendation."

"But she shot you."

"It was an accident," Nick insisted.

"So that's a no, then. You have no interest in pressing charges?"

Was the man on a witch hunt, or was this really standard procedure? "Is Ashleigh there now?" Nick asked.

"She'll be here in half an hour."

"I want to be there. I'm coming in," he said, which was easier said than done because he was stiff and sore and putting on pants could probably kill him.

"That's not really necessary," the officer said.

"Yes, it is, because you need to understand she didn't do anything wrong." Plus he wanted to see her again, and this was a perfect excuse because she might actually need him.

"Suit yourself," the officer said, and then he hung up without a goodbye.

Nick gritted his teeth as he bent over to retrieve a pair of underwear from his drawer, thinking how nice it was to have clothes in his drawer and not strewn all over his room. He had good intentions about keeping things clean, but he was so rarely at home. It was mainly a resting place between assignments. Thank goodness they had Melly to retrieve their mail or the place might look like an abandoned house most of the year.

His housemates were on base today, training because their assignment had been scrapped. That fact added to Nick's guilt because while he was home in bed, they were most likely in full gear, slogging through some swamp with their guns held aloft. The sergeant would take out his frustration on them, knowing it would indirectly get back to Nick when they came home exhausted.

Dressing himself was painful, but it was nothing compared to the ordeal of getting into his truck. Why had he bought this stupid, tall truck? Why couldn't he drive a car like normal people, something short he could slip into without having to hitch up his leg, which was proving impossible. Instead he sat on the edge of the truck and scooted inside before turning to crawl onto the seat. At least he was in the safety of the garage so no one was witness to his humiliation.

He was sweating profusely by the time he started the truck, and he still had to endure sitting on the seat, not to mention bouncing up and down as he drove down the road. What was wrong with his shocks? They didn't seem to be working at all this morning.

By the time he arrived at the police station, he was drenched in sweat. He wiped his face with the edge of his shirt and shimmied down from the truck. That, at least, was much easier than getting up had been. Ashleigh was sitting in the entryway, an older, distinguished-looking man to her right. Obviously it was her father because of course she had the type of family that would accompany her to the police station. Unlike Nick who'd had to walk home every time he had a run in with the police because not even when he was a kid could he find someone to care enough to pick him up from their local police station.

Ashleigh glanced absently toward the door and did a double take when she realized it was Nick. She stood and met him halfway across the room. Her hand reached out and stopped, suspended between them. "What are you doing here? You shouldn't be out of bed."

He suddenly felt foolish for thinking he was dashing to her rescue. Her father was there to take care of her; Nick's presence was unnecessary. She was smiling, though, as if she were as glad to see him as he was to see her. "They called and said they were interviewing you today. I thought you might need me." He trailed off, realizing how awkward he sounded, but Ashleigh's smile became exponentially brighter.

"That is so nice of you, especially since I know you must be miserable, and that's all my fault."

"Forget about it," he said. They were standing there, grinning at each other like idiots and probably would have continued if her father hadn't joined them and cleared his throat.

"How do you do, son? I'm Reverend Desmond." He held out his hand and Nick shook.

"Nick Lassiter, sir," Nick replied.

Reverend Desmond's eyes landed on Nick's wrist and traveled up his arm to the edge of his sleeve, no doubt taking in his tattoos. "You're in the marines?" he said it as a question, with incredulity.

"Yes, sir," Nick said, trying hard not to show how much the man's inspection was upsetting him. Of course he would only see an arm full of tattoos where his daughter's new friend was concerned. The problem was Nick didn't see himself much differently. He had gotten a tattoo for every epic event in his life, most of them bad. To him, the pictures on his arm represented failure and disappointment—one more reason he was no one's idea of a leader. "I see you're okay here, Ash, I should go."

"Don't be silly," Ashleigh said, resting her hand on his forearm. "I would love it if you could stay and walk me through this."

"It might help," Reverend Desmond said, though it clearly troubled him to have to admit it. "The detective sounded upset when he called. Having someone on our side might smooth things over." He paused, his eyes narrowing on Nick again. "You are on our side, aren't you?"

Nick saw where Ashleigh's bold, take-no-prisoners approach hailed from. "Yes, sir, I'm on your side. Ashleigh did the right thing."

The reverend nodded and looked away as if staring too long at Nick was painful for him. Ashleigh either didn't notice or didn't care because she was still beaming at Nick like his appearance was her greatest wish come true.

"How bad was it after I left last night?" she asked.

"It was okay," he said, shrugging a shoulder. In truth, it had been pretty bad, but then it always was with Tisha. She had a good heart, buried deep beneath all the layers of hurt and anger. Her first reaction to anything was always rage, as it had been at the sight of Ashleigh the previous evening.

The other guys began furiously shoveling their cobbler into their mouths as soon as Ashleigh left in a mad attempt to finish before Tisha's explosion. It didn't work.

"Who was she, Nick?" she screamed almost as soon as the door closed on Lolly and Ashleigh.

"She's who I said she is, Tish. We met today at the coffee shop, and she accidentally shot me."

"So, what, you brought her back here to rub it in my face your new snobby witch cooks for you?"

"She's not snobby or a witch," Nick said, immediately regretting the words when Lolly and Kelsey picked up their bowls and retreated to their rooms. Truck remained, but he shook his head at Nick's stupidity.

"Oh, excuse me. Your new little toy is as sickly sweet as this cobbler junk she made." She picked up the spoon from the bowl of cobbler Ashleigh had given her and threw it against the opposing wall.

"Hey!" Nick yelled, and as he did so he realized he and Tisha always resorted to yelling. It was their fallback form of communication, and all of a sudden he was tired of it. Exhausted, really.

He slumped, pushing aside his half-eaten cobbler. "Ashleigh is a nice person who was trying to make amends for shooting me. That's all." He purposely lowered his tone, his words soft and gentle. To his dismay it had an even worse effect on Tisha because she started to cry.

That was when Truck abandoned ship. Screaming he could handle—tears, not so much.

"I don't want to lose you," Tisha said.

Nick leaned over, wincing as he put his arms around her. "You're not losing me, Tish. It was one meal."

She swiped at her eyes. "Want me to stay tonight?"

He shuddered, thinking of her reaction if she saw the sheets Ashleigh had bought for his bed. "Thanks, but I'm tired, and I think I'll need to spread out tonight."

"Okay," she said. She plucked a peach from his bowl and ate it, grimacing as she swallowed. "It's too sweet."

Nick didn't say anything because he didn't agree. It wasn't too sweet; it was perfect.

"I've lost you," Ashleigh said, jogging him back to the present.

"Supper was really good last night," he said.

She laughed, a sweet bubbly sound that made his heart wrench for some reason. "You really were a million miles away."

He smiled. "The food was so good. I can't stop thinking about it."

He tried and failed to say it flippantly because what he really meant was he couldn't stop thinking about her.

"Then by all means have some more. Come home with me when this is over. My mother will cook a meal that will put mine to shame."

Nick opened his mouth—to say what, he didn't know—but the door opened and Sargent Hart Stuck his head out. "Miss Desmond, we're ready for you."

Ashleigh followed the detective, her father and Nick bringing up the rear like two warring bodyguards. The detective led them to a small interview room, so small there were only three seats. Nick didn't mind standing. In fact, he was glad for the excuse not to have to try and sit on his aching behind. He leaned against the wall instead. He wasn't trying to look intimidating, but the detective glanced at him a few times, his eyes lighting on Nick's tattoos with unease.

"Miss Desmond, let's go over your version of events one more time," the detective said.

"I stopped in Starbucks yesterday to get a latte. I had finished a job the day before, and lattes are my celebratory treat."

"You're a carpenter, is that correct?" The detective's curled lip and raised eyebrow made it clear what he meant to say was, "You think you're a carpenter; isn't that cute?"

"I'm a carpenter," Ashleigh replied. While Nick's hands were clenched, his muscles taut, Ashleigh didn't even sound annoyed. He wondered if she encountered a lot of skepticism about her job. He thought it was awesome. He had always wanted to know how to build things, but had never had anyone to teach him.

"And then what happened?"

"I heard the man chamber a shot, and I caught sight of him in my peripheral vision. My hand was already in my bag, reaching for my wallet, so I grabbed my gun instead, turned it on him, and told him to drop his weapon. Then Nick attacked. I hadn't seen him approach, so I thought the blur of movement was the man getting ready to shoot. So I shot, only I hit Nick instead." She turned, offering up an apologetic smile to Nick.

"I pulled the application for your concealed carry permit," Detective Hart said. "It states you wanted to carry a gun for protection."

"Doesn't everyone who wants to carry a gun want it for protection?" Reverend Desmond said. His tone sounded as impatient as Nick felt.

"Yes, but not everyone has filed a complaint against her ex-boyfriend. I pulled that call, too, and there was no name listed for the boyfriend. It simply stated he was a marine." He glanced at Nick, his eyes narrowing. "I don't like people who abuse the concealed carry permit, Miss Desmond, and if I find out this is some sort of twisted game you two are playing, you can bet I'm going to throw the book at you."

Nick took a step away from the wall and Ashleigh spoke. "What?"

"You heard me," the detective said. "This all looks a little too suspicious to me. It seems like you two were having an on again, off again lover's quarrel and you used the little episode yesterday in the coffee shop to get some retribution."

The other three occupants of the room stared at him like he was out of his mind. That he could come up with something so far out in left field was worrisome, especially because it almost sounded plausible, at least to Nick. He and Ashleigh hadn't been acting like two people who had just met. He could see how it might look like they had more going on than met the eye. He opened his mouth to defend Ashleigh, but she spoke for herself once again.

"I never met Nick before yesterday. My only goal was trying to neutralize the man with the sawed-off shotgun. I apologize for whatever woman gave you the idea a female of the species might use such a tense and volatile situation to gain revenge on a boyfriend, but I can assure you it's not true. Even if Nick had been my ex, I would never have shot him. Besides, my ex-boyfriend isn't here anymore. He's at Quantico. I would be happy to give you his name, but I would prefer you keep your questions from being inflammatory because I am, in fact, afraid of him." Her words sounded strong, but Nick noticed her lower lip quiver and had to fight the impulse to go to her and wrap his arms around her. Fortunately her father did it, preempting what would have been madness on his part.

"Detective, we're done here. My daughter has answered your questions and braved your suspicion and cynicism, but I won't allow you to wrongfully accuse her anymore. If you have further questions, then you can contact our lawyer. And you'd better believe I will be talking to your superiors about this little interview."

The detective seemed to be backpedaling now as he realized how off track his assumption had been. "We take our concealed carry laws and gun crimes very seriously," he said, holding up his hands palms out in surrender. "I simply want to make sure everything is above board. I apologize if I offended."

Reverend Desmond nodded, keeping his arm around Ashleigh as he led her out of the interview room. Now that it was over, she looked a little dazed. Nick followed behind them, pausing in the lobby when Ashleigh turned to him.

"Will you come?" she asked. Her face grew even paler when she was upset, her freckles standing out in stark relief. Her eyes were luminous and he felt as if there was no way he could say no to her, even if he wanted to.

"I'll come," he said, smiling when she smiled.

"Dad, I'll ride with Nick," she said, turning her smile on her father who didn't smile in return.

"Ashleigh, I'm not sure that's such a good idea. The officer thinks you two are dating."

"But we're not, and I'm not going to pretend or hide to appease an officer who has the wrong assumption," Ashleigh said. Some of the color returned to her face as her voice regained its normal steely conviction.

Reverend Desmond sighed, darting Nick another worrisome glance. "All right," he agreed at last. "I'll see you at home."

Ashleigh turned beaming back to Nick as her father walked away. "That was pretty horrible, huh?"

It took him a second to realize she was referring to the interview and not her father's reaction to him. "Yes, it was. Are you okay?"

"I'm fine." The way she said the words made it sound like she was trying to convince herself. They walked side by side in silence to his truck and then she grabbed his arm, halting him. "Oh, Nick. You poor guy. This is your car?"

His first reaction was to be offended—after all, the old truck had some dings—but then he realized she was talking about the height and the obvious difficulty he had getting in and out of it.

"I'm afraid so," he said, sighing dramatically. "Next time I buy a vehicle, I'm going to keep in mind the possibility I might get shot in the butt. I'll buy a low rider, something that drags the ground."

Ashleigh laughed and Nick's heart did the wrenching thing again. He couldn't tell if the sound of her laughter brought him pleasure, pain, or something in between. "I'm so sorry. At least let me help you inside."

"It's okay; I've got this," he said.

"It's funny how you thought that was a request," she said. She opened his door and turned to survey him, trying to figure out the best way to get him inside. Then she stooped, wove her fingers together, and held out her hand. "Let me be your step ladder."

"No way. I'm too big for you," he said.

"I'm a carpenter; I'm stronger than I look. Do it. I can hold you, I promise." She looked so determined and intent he had no heart to refuse her, so he put his foot in her hands, grimacing when he lifted his leg. She was a strong little thing because not only did she hold him, she also launched him into the seat so he landed hard on his stomach, breathless from the surprise and impact.

"Did I hurt you?" she asked, leaning over him in concern, her front pressed to his back as she attempted to see his face.

"Only my pride," he said. "Seriously, are you some sort of power lifter?"

"Nah, but I do a lot of heavy lifting on the job. It's nice because I don't have to work out. I can basically eat whatever I want and still maintain. I love my job." The last part was so heartfelt and enthusiastic he smiled, even though he still faced the difficult task of sitting up and driving home. "Why don't you let me drive?" she suggested.

"That way you can scoot over and you won't have to work the pedals."

He wanted to refuse because it was his truck and because he didn't like the thought of a woman driving him. But he was weak and in pain, and he knew it would make her feel better to be able to do something for him. Also, she had already held his hands while he had a bullet dug out of his posterior. How much more embarrassed could he get in her presence? "Okay," he said at last, inching across the seat like a caterpillar. Ashleigh hopped up and adjusted the seat, pulling it as far forward as it would go before taking his keys and starting it up.

"I have a truck, did you know?" she said. There was a combination of pride and hesitation in her voice that puzzled him. He understood the pride part; it went with the territory of owning a truck. But why was she embarrassed?

"I suppose you need it for your job," he said.

"I do, but I like it." She glanced at him. "Some men find it a turnoff I am into masculine things, as if that somehow makes me masculine. But I'm not. I'm a girly girl. I love dresses and nail polish, jewelry, and makeup. I also happen to like guns, trucks, and routers. I can be both."

"Of course you can," Nick said.

She glanced at him again, relaxing slightly. "You're all man," she said.

He would have laughed except she seemed to be asking him a question, and he didn't know what it was. "I hope so," he said.

"I mean, you don't seem to have tapped into your soft side. You don't cook or, I don't know. I don't even know what I'm trying to say. Usually when I'm near men whom I would describe as alpha males, no offense, they seem to be intimidated by the fact that I can open my own jar of pickles, if you know what I mean."

Nick thought that over for a minute before speaking. "Then I would say they aren't as secure in their masculinity as they seem. Their alpha maleness is a show, like the little wolf trying to make himself look bigger. Why should a true man care if you can open your own pickles? If that's the only thing he can do for you, he has bigger problems."

She stopped at a light and turned her gaze fully on him. "I think you may have summed up all my problems with dating in that one paragraph. Thank you." She reached over to pat his leg, withdrawing her hand quickly. He wondered if she felt the same spark of heat he did when they touched.

"So, the ex-boyfriend," he said when she started driving again. "He was a marine?"

She nodded, her lips pressed firmly together.

"I take it that didn't go well."

She shook her head.

"This is the point where you tell me the story and I stop trying to painfully drag it out of you," he said.

She let out a breath she probably didn't know she had been holding. The mention of the ex made her tense, apparently. "I wasn't one of those girls who was fascinated by marines. Growing up here, seeing them day in and day out around town, I sort of went the opposite direction and swore I would never date a marine. All that testosterone and cockiness, you know?" She darted him a glance before remembering she was talking to one of the said cocky, testosterone-filled marines. "Anyway, Charlie zeroed in on me and pursued me hard. I was nineteen to his twenty four, which should have been a red flag. But he was handsome, charming, and funny. And I fell for him.

"At first, everything was good. It was such a switch from my dating experiences in high school. Guys didn't like me once they got to know me. I'm, well, you know how I am. Sort of a bulldog when I set my mind on something. But Charlie liked that, or at least he seemed to. Things changed so subtly I didn't notice at first. His jokes started being at my expense. His possessiveness knew no bounds. Then it switched to outright verbal abuse. And I still didn't run away screaming. It was like my mind was warped."

"Did he hit you?" Nick asked, and now he was the one who was tense.

"A few times."

"Is that why you broke up?"

She shook her head. "I'm a virgin," she blurted, shocking him with her boldness. "At first, Charlie was gung ho with that idea. He liked that I was, in his words, old fashioned. Little did I know he had hopes of convincing me to let him be my first. That started subtle too, pressuring me to go past my comfort zone. When I refused, he laughed it off. At first. Then he became angry. This one time..." She broke off, swallowing.

"What?" he asked, his stomach clenching with an idea of what was coming.

"This one time he was angry when I said no. He tried to rape me. I barely got away, and that was the end. I ran to my dad, told him everything, and we went to talk to the police. Only there was the issue of him being a marine, and you guys having your own court system. Charlie was a golden boy. He's in Officer Candidate School now. There was a lot of pressure, a lot of insinuation that I asked for it, that I had it coming. So I let it go and he transferred to Quantico. Not without a few threats, though."

"What kind of threats?" he asked.

"That if I ever tried to pursue legal matters again, he would kill my family and make it look like an accident."

Nick swore. "Sorry," he muttered. But he couldn't believe it. Not only had her ex gotten away with it, but that it sounded as if the corps had helped him. "And that's why you got a gun."

"That's one of the reasons." She bit her lip, deciding if she wanted to tell him the next part.

"What?"

"A few weeks ago, I thought I saw him in town, watching me. It was far away and he was in the shade, but I think maybe it was him."

Nick started to swear but caught himself and changed it midword. "Fudge," he said instead, and Ashleigh laughed.

"That's the first time you've ever said that in your life, isn't it?" she asked.

"No. Sometimes at Christmas I say, mmm, fudge." Nick said.

Ashleigh patted his leg again. "You don't have to change for me, Nick. I like you the way you are."

He caught her hand, holding it before she could snatch it away again, but it didn't matter. They were at her house. "We're here," she announced. "Please don't tell my family about me possibly seeing Charlie. They don't know, and I don't want to worry them. It was a bad time after the breakup. I was...not myself. But I went to counseling for a few months, and things have been really good lately. I don't want them to regress to the state of constant paranoia."

"Your secret is safe with me," he said.

"Good. Now let's go meet the other Desmonds."

CHAPTER 8

"Ashleigh, he's perfect. I can't believe you brought me a marine."

"Caleigh, that joke wasn't funny the first time you said it a half hour ago, either," Ashleigh said to her little sister.

"Who says I'm joking?" Caleigh said. She stared at Nick with big green eyes framed by long dark lashes. Her hair was darker than Ashleigh's and she had the same smattering of freckles across her nose. Nick had been surprised to learn she was eighteen because she looked and seemed much younger.

"She's a young eighteen," Ashleigh had said, as if reading his thoughts.

"Ash, you make me sound like I'm twelve," Caleigh said, frowning at her sister.

"That's what you act like most of the time, and before you get angry let me assure you I mean that in the best possible way. Stay sweet and innocent forever, little one."

Caleigh rolled her eyes. "Yes, because you're so mature at twenty two."

"I'm more mature than I want to be," Ashleigh replied. "Which is why you are never allowed to date, ever, and especially not marines. No offense, Nick."

"Oh, how could I take offense at that?" Nick asked. He resisted the urge to reach out and put her in a playful chokehold, instinctively knowing any touch would only add to the potent mix of chemicals bouncing between them. But the missed opportunity left him staring at her, probably looking as soulful as Lolly when he was thinking over an issue.

"I know what you're thinking," Ashleigh said.

"You do?" Nick asked. Was he that easy to read?

"You're thinking it's pretty lame I still live with my parents. But the last couple of years I've been pouring everything into my business. First I had to buy and outfit a truck, and then I had to invest in some tools. A carpenter is only as good as her tools, and good tools are expensive. So my parents have generously been allowing me to live here until I build up my business and can afford to move out. And that day will be here soon."

"I wasn't thinking that at all," Nick said, though he wisely refrained from telling her what he had been thinking. "And if I lived here, it would probably take explosives to get me to leave." The house wasn't like any he had ever seen in real life. It wasn't grand, but it was cozy and homey. He would bet every bed in this house had sheets on it. It was clean and decorated with family pictures and vases of fresh flowers in every room. Nick had watched shows on television that depicted huge, stellar homes with tons of space and the latest technology, and he had mistakenly thought that was his dream. But this house, small, cozy, filled with love and good scents was revising his opinion. "Where's your workshop?"

"In the garage. Do you want to see?"

He didn't understand her hesitant tone. "Of course. Lead the way." He followed her to the garage and began to understand some of her hesitancy. It was intimidating to see the two rows of neatly lined tools and understand not only did he not have any idea how to use them, he didn't even know what they were called. Ashleigh did, however, and began picking them up, turning them over as if to check and make sure they were all okay.

"I've never used power tools," he admitted.

She glanced up in surprise, smiling. "You want to?"

"Can I?" he asked.

"Of course. I have some scraps over here; I'll show you what each one does, and you can have a go."

There were a lot of saws, and each one had a different name and purpose. Nick gave up trying when he couldn't remember which was the jig and which was the scroll. The table saw was his favorite. It ripped through large pieces of wood with raw power, giving him the same sort of rush he felt when he fired his sniper rifle. Ashleigh seemed to prefer the more detailed pieces, the planer and chisels.

"What exactly do you do for people?" Nick asked. He moved aside a stack of newspapers, thought better of it, and sat on the newspapers, enjoying the extra padding. He was in pain, but it was a bearable amount as long as he didn't think about it too much.

"Whatever they need me to do. Right now I do small custom jobs—some built-ins, closets, and pantries. Eventually I would like to branch out to do bigger jobs like kitchen renovations or maybe go the other direction and make furniture. I'm still new at this, still getting my feet wet and trying to decide my path. I'm on my own, working based on word-of-mouth recommendations. It would help me a lot if I could get in with some contractors and builders. But they're reticent to trust me."

"Because you're a woman?" he guessed.

"Yes."

"But why should that matter?"

She shrugged. "I don't know, but it does for some reason. Some blatantly tell me they don't think I can hack it in a man's world and some tell me they're afraid for my safety because construction is such a man's world."

Nick hadn't considered that aspect of things. "Have you had any trouble with that sort of thing?"

"Not more than any other woman."

"What does that mean?" he asked.

"It means men are men. Some whistle and make inappropriate comments. It's what men do."

"Not all men," he said.

"I know," she said. "See, I'm sometimes guilty of generalizing and stereotyping, too. Which is why I can't blame people for not giving me a chance because we're all guilty of it. I'm not worried though; I'll get there. Call me an optimist, but I believe hard work and character pay off. And, if not, then they provide their own reward."

"I happen to agree with you," he said.

"Then why don't you become an officer? I couldn't fail but notice Kelsey's not so subtle hint last night."

He looked away. "It's not for me," he said.

"Why not? Because you don't have a degree?" She knew from Charlie a four year degree was a requirement to become an officer.

"No, I got my degree going to school at night," Nick said.

"Then it sort of sounds like you were preparing yourself to be a candidate," she said. She sat cross-legged on a bench across from him. As soon as they arrived home she had changed into a faded t-shirt and jeans which did more to show off her very nice physique. Her arms were well toned without being bulky, and her waist was trim.

"I wanted to have the option," he said. "But I'm twenty seven."

"That leaves you a year."

"I forgot you're so well versed in all things marine," he said.

She smiled, but she was undeterred. "So what's the real reason, Nick? Why are you hedging? Obviously your team thinks you should go for it. Why don't you?"

What was it with her uncanny ability to cut to the chase? Nick had been dancing around that very question for as long as he had been in the corps. "I'm nobody's idea of a leader, okay?"

"But you're already a leader, aren't you? I was under the impression you're in charge of your team."

"I am, but that's different. That's three guys who know me. I've been trained to know what to do when we're in the field. They trust me because I've proved myself trustworthy. But giving orders to

Truck, Jaws, and Lolly is a whole lot different than giving orders to a battalion of strangers."

"Why?" she pressed.

"Because it is," he said. He tried and failed not to be annoyed by the conversation. Ashleigh had good intentions, but her bulldog nature didn't allow her to let things go.

"I'm trying to understand," she said gently. "I'm not trying to nag you."

"I know," he said. "It's a touchy subject, I guess."

She nodded, staring at her feet while she swung them gently back and forth. He wondered if he had offended her but apparently she was using the time to think up more questions. "How long have you and Tisha been dating?"

"A year," he said, suppressing a sigh. He didn't want to talk about himself or Tisha or the corps or anything else so far removed from her world.

"A year is a long time. Is it serious?"

"I suppose it depends on your definition," he replied.

"Are you going to marry her?"

"Not any time soon. I guess if we're still together in a few years we probably will." Unless Tisha figured out a way to get pregnant and make him marry her before then. Nick had long suspected she was trying to do exactly that, which was why he didn't trust her to cover birth control. She said she was on the pill, but he took his own precautions. Of course he couldn't explain any of this to Ashleigh-the-virgin. He felt guilty thinking it in her presence.

"Where did you meet?"

"A bar," he said, waiting to see if she would wrinkle her nose or shake her head or do anything else that reflected her disapproval, but she didn't. She nodded, biting her lip.

"Do you love her?" she spoke the words softly, hesitantly and Nick experienced that odd hitching in his chest again.

"I don't think I know what love is, Ashleigh." He had never seen it played out in front of him. How could he know whether or not he was feeling it for Tisha if he didn't know what it was?

"I don't think I do, either," Ashleigh said. "I thought I loved Charlie, but love's not supposed to be ugly. It's not supposed to break you."

"Isn't it?" Nick said. "What about that old adage that love hurts?"

She shook her head. "No, I mean I guess I do know what love is because it's a reflection of God. But I don't know what it feels like. I don't know how to find it."

"What do you mean about it being a reflection of God?" he asked.

"There's a verse in Corinthians that tells us what love is supposed to look like. Love is kind, patient, never envious or boastful, endures all things, hopes all things, and rejoices in the truth. I know for a fact that wasn't what I had with Charlie. It wasn't kind or patient, there was no hope or rejoicing, and the only endurance was on my part."

"You really believe all that stuff the bible says?" Nick asked. "You don't think it was some book written a long time ago by a bunch of guys?"

"I do believe that, but I also believe it was inspired by God and I believe it's stood the test of time. More than my belief is my experience, though. Before Charlie I believed, but it's different now that I've been through something so painful. My faith has been tested and proved true."

"You sound like Lolly," Nick said.

"Lolly's a nice guy," Ashleigh said.

"He's a sweet kid," Nick said. He chuckled and shook his head. "Listen to me—he's a year older than you and I talk about him like he's a baby. But he's so innocent and *nice.* He's definitely our team conscience, but he does it in a good way, you know? Not preachy or shoving it down our throats. He's always quietly there, being so pure it makes us want to be better in comparison."

"That's the best way," Ashleigh said. "The preachy stuff doesn't work. You might not believe this, but I went through a phase where I tried it. I was sort of a bulldog back then. I've mellowed."

"If this is you mellow, I'm not sure I want to meet the before you. I'd probably run away screaming."

"You probably would," she said. "I was dogmatic, and it was such a turnoff. I regret that. If there's one thing good that came out of my relationship with Charlie it's that my brokenness led to a softer heart and more humility. I understand now what it means to struggle with things, to hurt so deeply you're not sure where to turn. I didn't get that before, growing up in my sheltered world where everything is black and white. The world's a better place when you open your eyes to the shades of gray."

"Whoa, deep," Nick said. His tone was light, but her words had resonated with him. He had pictured her world as perfect, but Ashleigh knew a little bit about pain. She wasn't going to judge him, and that knowledge went straight to his heart, settling deep. There was a chance that, despite their many differences, they might actually be friends.

"Yeah, I don't do lighthearted well. Sorry." She shook her head, her eyes landing on one of her saws. "I'm a female carpenter Christian virgin from an abusive relationship. Is it any wonder the men are beating a path to my door?" She glanced back at him with a wry, self-deprecating smile.

He didn't admit his own list of descriptors was easily as off-putting. "I'm here," he said instead.

"Yes, but you're special," Ashleigh said. "You have a heart as big as the moon."

He waited for the punch line, but it never came. "I don't get it," he said at last.

"Get what?"

"The joke," he said.

"I wasn't joking. I think you're one of the nicest guys I've ever met."

He stared at her again. "Me?"

"Yeah, you." She pointed at his chest for good measure. "It's the eyes. They radiate kindness and warmth and intelligence and..." she trailed off, biting her lip to stop her errant flow of words. "You have nice eyes, Nick," she finished lamely, hopping off the table. "Let's go see what Mom is preparing for dinner."

He followed her back into the house where Ashleigh made the introductions to her mother, who was more like Caleigh both in looks in personality. Ashleigh and her father shared the same muddy green eyes, chestnut hair, and take-no-prisoners personality while Caleigh and Mrs. Desmond had darker hair, greener eyes, and bubblier personalities. In the mother, Nick sensed none of the disapproval he had felt from Reverend Desmond.

"I'm so glad you could join us today, Nick. I always make too much food. Ash, why don't you show him where the bathroom is so he can get washed up and then maybe you two can help me finish some things up."

"Sure, Mom," Ashleigh replied. They turned toward the door when Mrs. Desmond called them back.

"Oh, and a letter came for you today. It's on the counter."

Ashleigh grabbed it as she passed, tearing it open without paying attention to what it contained. "Here's the bathroom," she said. She followed him inside as she glanced at the paper in her hands. Nick turned on the water and then turned it off again when he caught sight of her pale face in the mirror.

"Ashleigh, what is it?" he asked.

She opened her mouth to answer, but no sound came out. He plucked the letter from her frozen fingers and read the chilling words for himself. "I'LL KILL YOU."

CHAPTER 9

"*P*lease, Nick, please don't say anything." Ashleigh plucked the note from Nick and stuffed it in her pocket.

"Ashleigh, this isn't the kind of thing you should keep from your parents," Nick said, though who was he to give advice? He hadn't spoken to his mother in two years. Her family situation was much different than his, though.

"You promised," Ashleigh whispered.

"I promised not to mention you may or may not have seen your ex who is stationed in Quantico. This is different. This is definitive."

"Please, Nick. You have no idea what it was like after Charlie, how worried they were. This is his M/O. He strikes when I least expect it and tries to keep me afraid, but I refuse to live my life in fear. He's a bully, and I won't let him have control over my life anymore. If I tell Mom and Dad, then he wins because they'll worry. The cycle will start all over again. I'm going to forget this and pretend it never happened." She reached to throw the envelope in the trash, but he preempted her and looked it over.

"Ashleigh, this stamp wasn't canceled. This letter was hand delivered," Nick said.

She shrugged. "It's not like he's never been to the house before. Of course he knows where I live."

"Yes, but…"

He would have said more, but she reached out and rested her hand lightly on his forearm. "It's really no big deal. Let's forget it and have a nice evening, okay?" She was wearing the look, the one that said resistance was futile, and he smiled.

"Does anyone refuse an order from you and live to tell the tale?"

"Caleigh. The child disobeys me at every turn. Drives me crazy." Her hand was still on his arm, her thumb smoothing gently back and forth. He looked down and she followed the line of his gaze, jerking her hand away. "Sorry," she said. "I'm not trying to hit on you. It's just…" She trailed off and gave a helpless little shrug.

It's just that you want to touch me as badly as I want to touch you, he thought. Their attraction was as potent as it was baffling. He had never felt such an intense physical chemistry with someone before, and especially not someone who was off limits on so many different levels. Even now as all the reasons for not touching her ran through his mind, all he wanted to do was put his hands on her waist, lean in, and kiss her. If it had been anyone else, he would have given in to the impulse, Tisha or no Tisha. But it wasn't some woman; it was Ashleigh who was pure and innocent and who had already been irreparably damaged by another marine. He felt he owed it to the corps to make up for the other guy who came before. And the only way to do that was to not touch her. It was a maddening catch-22. They had no future, but he couldn't simply use her and walk away because she was the type of woman who required a future. The best course of action was to leave now and never see her again.

But he didn't do that, either. He followed her out of the bathroom and to the kitchen where they chopped vegetables, talking and laughing with her mother like they hadn't almost kissed in the bathroom, like she hadn't received a death threat in the mail.

Reverend Desmond joined them at the table, his grim expression becoming grimmer at the sight of Nick. Ashleigh was subdued over supper, allowing her sister and mother to carry the conversation with their bubbly chatter.

"Where are you from, Nick?" Mrs. Desmond asked as soon as the prayer was over. Nick was congratulating himself on remembering to wait for grace before reaching for the food this time.

"I'm from all over," Nick said, his tone purposefully vague.

"Were your parents in the armed forces?" she asked.

"No, ma'am," Nick replied. His mother had been a drifter, pawning him on whatever family and friends would take him. Once he had tried to count how many schools he had attended, but gave up trying after he topped a hundred and fifty.

"Do you kill people?"

"Caleigh," Ashleigh exclaimed, shooting her little sister a look.

"What?" Caleigh asked. "He's a soldier. It's a logical question."

"Logical, maybe. Tactless and rude, definitely," Ashleigh said.

"I was only asking," Caleigh said, her face scrunching into a pout. She was a remarkably pretty child, and even though she was legally an adult, Nick thought of her as a child. If possible, she was even more innocent than Ashleigh. "Sorry," she added, noting Nick's continued silence.

He smiled at her, but didn't reply. His kills weren't something he talked about ever, with anyone, not even his own teammates. It was his job and better for all concerned if he left it at that, compartmentalizing his complex emotions.

"Ashleigh told us about your teammates," Mrs. Desmond said. "I would love to meet them. Our church is always looking to adopt soldiers."

Nick didn't say so, but he thought that sounded great. None of them had any family connections except Lolly, and Melly's packages always came with the instruction not to let Kelsey touch them, although she always sent along his favorite candy and cookies. But Melly was busy and she was only one woman. She couldn't always keep up when they went on long deployments, which thankfully wasn't very often.

"Shouldn't you be stationed with a battalion somewhere?"

Reverend Desmond asked. His tone indicated his hope Nick would say yes and go there now.

"There are different kinds of reconnaissance teams," Nick said, carefully sidestepping his job so as not to give them too much information. "Some are stationed with battalions, and some work directly for the Department of Defense." He wondered if they would understand what he wasn't saying, that sometimes the government needed small teams that could slip under the radar when they were sent places they weren't supposed to be. He and his team were invisible, getting in and out of countries without anyone ever knowing they were there. Except for the dead body left behind, the one with an M40 bullet hole in it that basically served as a marine calling card.

"Are you a spy?" Caleigh asked.

"Yes," Nick said. "But a lot of marines are. We work in reconnaissance; that means retrieving information. Some of us are better at it than others. I'm good, but my teammate Lolly is the best. I've never seen anything like him; he's a ghost in the field."

"The advantage of being small," Ashleigh said.

Nick nodded. "His size certainly helps him remain undetected. He can get in a lot of places the rest of us can't, and he can hide better, too. Kelsey and I are so tall we have to rely on other means of camouflage."

"You have a ghillie suit?" Reverend Desmond asked. He sounded interested, albeit grudgingly.

"Yes, sir. It's taken me years to perfect my suit, to get the right amount of dirt stains and odor."

"You want it to smell?" Mrs. Desmond asked, her nose wrinkled in disgust.

"Yes, ma'am, because wild odors like swamp, animal feces, and decay are natural odors. Human sweat, shampoo, and detergent are not. A trained scout notices scents. Someone who knows what he's doing would be able to smell deodorant a half mile away. We have to be conscious of all aspects of disguise, even our heat imprint because everyone has an infrared sensor these days."

They were blinking at him in unison and Nick realized he was taking this family down a path they shouldn't go. They were the sort of people he liked to think he was protecting when he was in the field —innocent, hard-working Americans who made the world a better place. They shouldn't have to know there were people like him who did what he did for a living. They should remain in ignorance, going about their daily lives blissfully unaware of the cesspool around them. He focused on his food and began eating in earnest. Ashleigh caught his eye and smiled, almost as if she knew what he was thinking. He wondered if maybe she did, and the thought she might eased a little of the pervasive loneliness inside him.

No doubt about it, he and this woman shared some kind of connection, a thought that both intrigued and depressed him. Why should he have anything in common with someone so different was odd, even if all they shared was some sort of attraction to each other. But the thought that it didn't matter because he couldn't act on and explore their chemistry was depressing.

Supper finished and Ashleigh led him to a small den off the kitchen. There was a couch and a television. Ashleigh pointed to the couch. "Lie down," she commanded.

"I'm good," Nick said. He felt odd about lying on a stranger's couch, mostly because lying down was a position of submission, and he didn't want to feel any more vulnerable than he already did. Being here in this place so far removed from normal already made him feel off-kilter, to say nothing of what being near Ashleigh did to him.

"Nick, I know you have to be in pain, and it makes me feel horrible. Please lie down for a few minutes and rest. Please." She clasped her hands together, her muddy green eyes going all soft as if granting this one request would mean the world to her. Nick sighed because he was a goner when she looked at him like that and said please. He lay on his stomach and she sat beside him, her body scrunched close to the arm to give him maximum space.

The moment his body touched the couch, he knew it was a mistake because all of his energy was suddenly gone. He hadn't realized until he stopped moving how tired and sore he was, but now inertia was taking over, and he was afraid he might never get up again, a feeling that wasn't helped when Ashleigh began smoothing her hand gently over his head.

"You want to know something?" she said.

"Hmm," he replied. His hand eased up and rested on her knee because if she was going to touch him, then it was only fair he touch her in return.

"I dated Charlie for over a year, and I never respected what it means to be a marine until tonight at the table. I had no idea what it must be like to do what you do, but tonight I was picturing it, picturing you guys in the field, wearing your ghillie suits with Lolly ghosting around undetected."

His hand tensed on her knee. "I don't want you to think about it, Ashleigh. I shouldn't have mentioned anything about my job."

"It's okay to share what you do with me, Nick. I think I understand more than you realize about it. And I know it's a secret. I would never say anything to anyone. I didn't tell Mom and Dad about you being a sniper. And, this is going to sound corny, but I have to say it: I'm really proud of you."

It didn't sound corny, it sounded wonderful, like healing words that went to his soul and did a little repair work on some of the damage life had done. He didn't reply because his throat felt constricted, and he didn't want to embarrass himself with an emotional display.

"This is the part where I sing the national anthem," Ashleigh said.

Nick laughed, glad for the reprieve from serious topics. Her hand shifted slightly and began tracing his ear with her thumb. She sighed. "I should not be doing this. It's like feeding an addiction. I'm not normally the woman who throws common sense out the window. You and I, we're all wrong."

"Yes," Nick agreed. "I should go." But he didn't go, and Ashleigh didn't stop touching him. Instead he shifted closer so his head was lying in her lap and she covered him with an afghan. He felt warm and safe and right somehow, as if he had finally found a home. Maybe it was the effect of being in a home, one with decorations and pictures and a family who loved each other. He told himself that was what it was because it couldn't be the woman beside him. It had to be the well-appointed house and cozy atmosphere. Maybe if he had a nice house with nice things, then he would feel his same pervasive peace with Tisha. But not even thoughts of his girlfriend could force him to move away from Ashleigh and her gentle, soothing touch on his head.

CHAPTER 10

Four hours later, they were still operating under the pretense Nick was going to go home at any minute. Even though it was midnight and he was still lying on the couch. And even though Ashleigh had moved to the floor and was no longer touching him, the palpable intimacy still hovered between them, cocooning them so they felt like they were isolated from the world.

Nick was still lying facedown on his stomach and Ashleigh was lying on the floor beside the couch, looking up as they talked. For a while, they had watched television, but Ashleigh kept interrupting with snippets of conversation until at last their conversation had taken over any illusion of watching TV, so they turned it off and started to talk in earnest.

"Tell me again why you don't want to be an officer," Ashleigh commanded.

"What do you mean again? I didn't tell you the first time."

"So tell me now," she said, smiling. "And you should know if you don't, I'm going to keep bugging you until I eventually wear you down. Might as well give in now and save us both the time and effort."

"I'm not officer material," Nick said. "You can't be like me and be the guy possibly thousands of people look to for direction."

"What do you mean like you?" Ashleigh said. "What's wrong with you?"

"Nothing. I wasn't made to be an officer, that's all."

"Why not?" Ashleigh said, and he realized then she meant what she said. She would keep pecking and pecking until she got to the heart of the matter and he told her what she wanted to know, so he might as well give in and do it now.

He sighed. "My mom had me when she was sixteen. I have no idea who my father is, and neither does she because the possible list of candidates is so long. She considers herself a free spirit, which makes it all the weirder she felt like she wanted to be tied down by a baby. Or maybe she didn't, because she never let me tie her down. Sometimes I lived with her, and sometimes I lived with one of her friends or cousins or boyfriend's parents. Whoever she could find to take me for a couple of months."

She reached for his hand, twining her finger through his to give it a sympathetic squeeze. "I'm sorry."

He smiled and pulled her hand closer, tucking it under his chin. "It probably sounds worse than it is. Some of those people were nice and interesting. It wasn't as if I was ever abused. But sometimes neglect is its own kind of demon because I had no supervision, no continuity. I did whatever I wanted, whenever I wanted. I took my first drink at eight, smoked my first joint at nine. I tried cigarettes, but didn't like the taste. I lost my virginity when I was eleven, got my first tattoo when I was fourteen. I've lived everywhere, done everything. I'm twenty seven, and I'm exhausted by life. What could I possibly have to offer as an officer?" He hadn't meant to unload quite so much. There was a part of him that feared her censure, but there was another, bigger part of him that understood there wouldn't be any judgment from her. Either he was beginning to know her or trust her or both.

She studied him in silence a few beats, her pale face looking even paler as the night wore on. "Do you know what I see when I look at you, Nick?"

"What?" he asked, whispering to match the gravity in her tone.

"I see a man who has lived a hard life and yet somehow thrived, despite the odds. You could have been a statistic. You could be dead or a druggie or a gang member. Instead you pulled yourself up by your bootstraps and found a career, and not any career. You're the most elite of the elite, the special forces of the toughest military branch on the planet. And it's not only that—it's you. You're magnetic without being cocky, a leader without being controlling. I saw it the moment I met you, the take charge nature tinged with a heavy dose of kindness and compassion. Do you have any idea how rare and special you are? You would be the kind of commander a young recruit dreams of because you've been there; you've been in his shoes. You weren't born with a military pedigree and Ivy League education. You've earned every ding and battle scar, and you know how to help the young guy you were. If I were sending my son to join the marines, I would pray and beg God for an officer like you."

He had no reply to what was undoubtedly the nicest thing anyone had ever said to him. Instead he rubbed his stubbly cheeks gently over her hand as she traced the outline of his crooked nose.

"What happened there?" she whispered.

"Hockey. I spent a winter in Northern Minnesota in high school. There wasn't much else to do, but it taught me how to fight dirty. Also chipped my tooth." He opened his mouth and used his tongue to point to his broken tooth.

"Your face has character," she said. "I like it."

"Is that a nice way of saying I'm ugly?" he asked.

"Don't fish for compliments; you know you're very handsome."

"C'mon, admit it: you've never been attracted to a guy like me in your life."

"Before now, you mean?" she asked.

"Miss Desmond, are you flirting with me?"

"Blatantly. What are you going to do about it?" she said.

"Not a thing," he replied, sighing.

"And that's why I like you, because you try to pretend you're some tough bad guy, but you're actually a sweetheart."

"I could fill a page with people who believe that's not true," he said.

"Would anyone who actually knows you be on that list?" she asked.

He had to pause and think about that. "I guess not," he said. The people who thought he was a streetwise thug were people who bought his act and didn't actually know him. "If I become an officer, I would have to get my tats removed," he said, staring absently at his picture-covered arm.

"Because of policy?"

"No. I was grandfathered in under the policy of no head or neck tattoos. They've since changed it to no sleeve tattoos. But can you imagine an officer looking like this?" He held out his arm for her inspection. She sat up and leaned closer, grasping his arm to turn it over.

"What's this one?" she asked, skimming her finger over a small heart.

"First time I thought I fell in love."

"This one." It was a picture of an open mouth, twisted in anger.

"First time my mother told me I was a mistake."

There was a picture of a sniper round, similar to the one he was wearing, and she ran her fingers over it, not asking what it meant. Somehow she knew it was a memento of his first kill. "Why would you get rid of these when they're a part of who you are?" she asked.

"They're not exactly professional," he said.

"Depends on the profession. If I saw a colonel with this many pictures on his arm, I would assume he had a compelling story to go along with his fancy title."

"Are you saying you want a tattoo?" he asked.

She smiled and let go his arm. "Not in a million years. But you have them, and they mean something to you. Don't let go of that."

"You have all the answers to life's biggest questions," Nick said.

"Is that a nice way of saying I'm opinionated?" she asked settling back against the carpet.

"No, it's a way of saying you're wise for someone so young. I know a lot of guys your age in the corps, and they've got nothing on you."

"I was this really dogmatic and opinionated kid. I thought I did know all the answers. Then life happened and now I realize I know nothing. Pain has a tempering effect; it makes you stronger and more malleable, proving you can be bent but not broken, providing you with a little wisdom along the way. Not that it's fun, but at least it makes you a better person."

"If you let it. Some people embrace bitterness and never learn what they're supposed to."

"Speaking of pain, how are you doing?"

"I'm fine."

"Nick, you haven't moved from that spot all night."

"It's a really comfy couch," he said.

"I'm going to get you some pain reliever," she declared.

"I'm fine, Ash. I should get home anyway."

"You're not going anywhere until I get you that pain reliever. Stay there." She pointed at him and sprinted away. She hurriedly retrieved some pain reliever and a glass of water, but he was already fast asleep by the time she returned. She stood looking at him for a few minutes before snapping to attention with a shake of her head. What was she doing staring at him like some sort of lovesick teenager? She had promised herself after Charlie she would be more careful, and yet here she was swooning over another beautiful marine.

Still, he didn't look very dangerous asleep. In fact, he looked sweet and innocent. In some ways, he was confident and in charge, but in other ways he didn't think very highly of himself, and that made her sad. A childhood of neglect and insecurity had done a number on him. She set the water and pain reliever on a coaster and resisted the urge to touch him again. She couldn't seem to help herself when she was near him. Nick was an interesting mix of steel and vulnerability, an enigma. How could someone who killed people for a living be so soft-hearted? But he was. She wasn't one to lose her heart easily, especially not after Charlie, but Nick was the most intriguing and attractive man she had ever met. Ashleigh had never been so tempted by anyone, and especially not someone who had a girlfriend.

Instead of rifling her fingers through his hair like she wanted, she instead found another cover and tucked it around him. "Goodnight," she mouthed, feeling pathetic and lovesick, worse than she had over her first crush as a thirteen year old. What she needed was to get a grip. Hopefully a good night's sleep would restore some sanity.

CHAPTER 11

"Nick."

The sound of someone whispering his name alarmed him and he jumped, wincing. How was it possible he hurt worse today than yesterday? *Because the doctor dug through muscle.* Muscle pain was always worse before it got better. His mouth was open, and he tasted unfamiliar twine when he closed it. This wasn't the fake leather sofa he shared with his teammates. This was the quality sofa at Ashleigh's house. Not only had he fallen asleep facedown like a drunk sleeping off a bender, but he had slept all night, if the faded early morning sunlight filtering through the windows was any indication.

"Nick, I have to go."

Nick couldn't manage to turn all the way over on his sore backside, so he settled for turning his head. Ashleigh was standing over him. She smiled and reached out to swipe her hand gently over his head.

"Where are you going?" he asked.

"I'm starting a new job today. I like to get an early jump on things." She paused, biting her lip before she continued. "I know you're dreading the boredom this week. I thought you might want to meet up with me and hangout, see what I do. If you want. No big deal if you don't."

"I want," he said. "Okay if I go home and grab a shower?"

She smiled. Was it possible she looked relieved, as if there had been any doubt he would say no to her invitation? "Sure. Sleep a few more hours here if you want. No one will disturb you."

"I'm up," he said.

"Sorry I woke you."

"Sorry I fell asleep on your parents' couch. I bet your dad loved that."

"He didn't mind," Ashleigh said.

Nick quirked an eyebrow at her. "He checked on me to make sure I was in my room and not cuddled up beside you," she said. "And *then* he didn't mind." They shared a smile while she continued to make passes over his skull. It was intensely soothing to be touched by her, an electrifying combination of comfort and attraction. What did she get out of it, he wondered. Must be something because she kept doing it.

"I really should go," she said. "I wrote down the address and put it by your glass of water and pain reliever. I'll see you."

"See you," Nick said. Maybe it was a good thing he could barely move because it kept him from reaching for her. Reluctantly, she pulled her hand away from him, gave him one last smile, and let herself out of the house.

He waited until she was completely gone before he attempted to go through the embarrassing routine of pulling himself up. He groaned as he reached for the pain reliever and address. Walking wasn't going to be fun today, and neither would riding in his truck, but then he saw a set of keys with an attached note.

"I took my work truck today; take my car. Please. Ashleigh." Her writing was loopier and girlier than he had expected. Ashleigh was such a straightforward, no-nonsense person he expected her to print in block letters like he did.

He made his way outside, hobbling like an old man, and then he stopped short, tipping his head to stare at the driveway. There were wet tire tracks behind his truck, but Ashleigh's truck had been parked in the back near the garage. He could clearly see where her truck drove out on the grass, and the tacks were wider than the tracks in the driveway. None of the other Desmonds were awake yet. Who could have left the tracks?

He scanned the house, driveway and mailbox, looking for the newspaper in case it had been a delivery person, but there was no paper. Nick felt uneasy, especially in light of Ashleigh's anonymous letter yesterday. Was someone watching her? Had they followed her?

He checked the address where he was supposed to meet her, but he had no idea where it was. He wanted to go home and shower, but he wasn't going to be easy until he checked on her, so he pulled out his phone and pushed in the number he had somehow already committed to memory.

"Hey," Ashleigh said. "Something wrong?"

Hearing her voice was reassuring, but also made him feel like a mother hen for his unnecessary worry. "Where is this place you're going today?"

"North, near Half Moon and the forest."

"Sounds remote."

"It's out there."

"Do you feel safe?" he asked.

"Sure. The owner works from home. He's not exactly a marine, but he could probably dial 911 if I accidentally cut off my finger."

It wasn't her having an accident he was worried about, but there was no need to tell her that. He would be with her soon enough, and then maybe the gnawing anxiety would leave his chest. "All right, I'll see you in a few."

"Take my car," she commanded.

"I'm fine," he said.

"Nick, please. I know you're hurting, and this is the one thing I can do for you. Please."

He squinched his eyes closed, knowing he was going to take her car. How could he refuse when she was being so sweet about it? "Fine," he agreed. "I'll see you in a few." They disconnected and he shimmied into her car. She was right; it was much easier than trying to lift himself into his own tall truck. He was so sore today he drove with his left foot to try and give his aching right side a break.

He arrived at his house and headed for the kitchen. The sooner he ate something, the sooner he could take more pain reliever. The only thing in the fridge was a half gallon of milk. It was probably Truck's, and he would probably freak if Nick drank it, but right now he didn't care. He made a mental note to buy Truck some more milk and then chugged straight from the carton for a few minutes. He finished, swiped the back of his hand over his mouth, and reached for the bottle of aspirin on the counter. Pain reliever was the one thing they kept well stocked because one of them was always dinged up or hung over or both.

"Whoa." Kelsey came into the kitchen and opened the fridge, staring at the empty shelves in dismay. He pulled out Truck's milk and chugged the rest of it. "I'm telling Truck it was you," he said as he crushed the empty container and tossed it onto the floor beside the overflowing trash can. He sat at the counter and surveyed Nick. "You just getting home?"

"Yep," Nick said.

"Whoa. That was fast work."

"What do you mean?"

"I mean I thought it would take longer to get into the PK's bed. I guess you can never tell with some people."

Nick scowled at him. "It wasn't like that. She lives with her parents and I crashed on their couch, far away from Ashleigh."

Kelsey held up his hands in surrender. "I wasn't criticizing; I was impressed."

"Don't be. It's not like that with her."

"What is it like? Because I've never seen you this way with anyone."

"We're friends, I guess. I've never really been friends with a woman before," Nick said.

"You're friends with Melly."

"Not like that. Melly and I are friends like I would be friends with any friend's sister. We've never had a conversation deeper than 'Hey, how you doing?'"

"Really? I talk to Melly all the time."

"That's because you're in love with her," Nick said.

Kelsey shook his head. "Don't try to turn this on me; we're talking about you. So you're friends. Friends doesn't explain your behavior lately."

"What behavior?" Nick asked.

"It's different with this girl. *She's* different."

"Tell me about it," Nick said.

"Okay, I will. Usually you meet a woman and the race is on to see how fast you can get her clothes off. You have zero chance of that happening with PK, and yet you're still into her. It's freaking me out."

"It's freaking me out, too," Nick said. He dropped his voice to a whisper and glanced furtively toward the stairs. "I feel like I'm turning into Lolly."

"Dude, don't say that; don't even joke," Kelsey said, shuddering. Lolly had a conscience which, in their opinion, made him no fun at all.

"I'm not joking," Nick said, still whispering. "The stuff I'm thinking lately is all the stuff Lolly says. It's like he's laid eggs in my head and they're hatching." He tapped his temple. "All I can think is how I want to take care of her and protect her from everything. And there's this feeling in my gut when I'm with her like…like coming home."

Kelsey stared at him, horrified. "Snap out of it," he said. "Seriously, get away from her. Maybe she's using some sort of Christian mind control on you. Don't see her again, and you'll forget about her."

Nick shook his head. "I'm seeing her again in a few minutes, after I shower."

"Are you crazy?" Kelsey thundered. "This girl is going to ruin your life if you let her."

Nick shrugged. "I think she's in trouble. She needs me."

"That's how it starts, Nick. She needs you today and then two years from now you're putting together a crib and inviting me over for a backyard BBQ."

Nick bent over and groaned as if Kelsey had jabbed him in the solar plexus.

"See? Freaky stuff."

"No, that's the problem. You said it, and I could picture it. I...I think I kind of want it."

Kelsey had no words. This wasn't what they had planned for their lives. Neither of them would even say the word "Marriage" until after they were thirty. They were only twenty seven and in their prime. Now Nick was talking like being tied down with one woman and a mortgage was somehow a good thing.

"Get over it," Kelsey said, infusing his voice with all the panic he felt. He couldn't lose his best friend--his brother--this way. Without Nick, he would truly be alone. He had Truck, Lolly, and Melly, but it wasn't the same as having Nick. The others had come later. Nick was the foundation on which his life now stood, the rock who was unchanging. If he changed, if he pulled away and married someone, where did that leave Kelsey? Alone. He had been alone before; he didn't want to be alone again.

Nick stood upright and let out a breath. "I gotta go. I don't like leaving her alone so long at her work site. I think someone followed her or maybe they were watching her. The point is I think she's in danger."

I don't care. Kelsey refrained from saying the words with difficulty, but he meant them. What was it to him some random woman was in danger? It was nothing, and it was nothing to Nick. He didn't know why he was making it his business when it wasn't. Why couldn't he simply forget this woman and concentrate on Tisha? Tisha wasn't always the most pleasant company, but she was safe. There was nothing about her that would threaten their way of life or upset the balance.

He watched Nick walk away and pulled out his phone, his thumb pressing his speed dial.

"What's wrong?" Melly answered.

"Why does something have to be wrong?" Kelsey asked.

"Because it's six thirty in the morning on a Monday. Is it Jesus?"

"Lolly's fine. What are you doing today?"

She paused as if trying to figure out where he was going with his question. "Teaching twenty kindergarteners all about the letter G. What are you doing?"

"Marching through a swamp in full gear. The sergeant is really steamed at Nick for getting shot."

There was a lull in conversation, but it was comfortable.

"What's wrong, Kelsey?" Melly pressed.

"Nothing, I...I need you to tell me things are always going to be the same."

"They're not."

"Thanks, Melly. I knew I could count on you to make me feel better," Kelsey said, heavy on the sarcasm.

"What do you want me to do, keep life from happening?"

"Yes," Kelsey said. "Could you please?"

"No. But the good news is while circumstances change, people rarely do, which in some cases isn't a good thing. Hint, hint."

"Wow, I am so glad I dialed you this morning."

She laughed, and he smiled. "The point is the people in your life will always be there for you to see you through the changes."

"But what if they're not?" What if they get married or die or move on?

"The people who love you, the people who really care about you, will always be there. I'll always be there. Jesus, Ashton, and Nick will always be there."

Somehow when she said it he believed her. The anxiety wriggling in his chest was quelled, at least for the moment. "Are you coming over later?"

"Jesus is going out with Ashton," Melly said. Ashton was attempting to teach the youngest marine how to pick up women, which was laughable since no one could remember the last time Truck had a date.

"You can't come to see me? I'm obviously in desperate need of reassurance here."

"I thought you had a date with Bitsy or Yipsy or whatever her name was."

"Bitty. I dumped her a couple of days ago. She was beginning to cling."

"Wow. You guys dated for like two weeks. I thought maybe she was the one."

"Yeah, I'm heartbroken and in desperate need of consolation. You coming?"

"You have to promise me vegetables. I cannot eat pizza or burgers one more night."

"What if we compromise and I get you a burger with a multivitamin?" he asked.

"I want something green."

"Lots of green stuff in our fridge," he said.

"Something that couldn't kill bacteria," she said.

"*Women*. Fine, I will buy you a salad."

"With chicken," she said.

"A salad with chicken."

"Which you will pay for because you owe me fifty bucks."

"What? Why do I owe you fifty bucks?" he asked.

"Bitsy wanted something and you were out of cash until payday."

"Oh, right. Next woman I date better be rich."

"Next woman you date better have an IQ higher than her age," Melly said.

"I don't discriminate."

"That's true—you are an equal opportunity jerk. It really annoys me there is this constant stream of women lining up to be used by you. Where's the self respect?"

"Said the lonely woman who begged me to buy her a salad."

"That's nowhere close to reality," Melly said. "But in your head reality is an illusion, so it will do no good to argue."

"Finally you're learning," Kelsey said.

"If I really learned, I would change my number and move. See you." She hung up and he tucked his phone in his pocket, whistling now as he started his day.

CHAPTER 12

The house where Ashleigh was working was in the middle of nowhere, surrounded by woods with a long, winding drive. It was every stalker's dream come true. If her ex found her out here, there would be no one to help, no one to hear her screams.

Nick gripped the steering wheel tighter and shifted to the left as he studied the house. The pain reliever had only taken the edge off. He was in misery, and sitting down was not his friend. Slowly, he slid out of the car and went to search for Ashleigh.

She wasn't hard to find. She had set up a work station outside the house, compete with sawhorses and a couple of saws. He stood back and watched her work, appreciating the way the muscles bunched in her sinewy arms. Well-defined muscles weren't something he had ever looked for in a woman before, but he might have to change that now because the strength in her petite figure appealed to him. Everything about her appealed to him, and that was the problem.

He waited to speak until she set down the saw and removed her earplugs. "Hey."

She spun and beamed at him, a smile that let him know she had been looking forward to his arrival, as if seeing the sun after a long absence. Had anyone ever been that glad to see him? Probably not.

Had it been like that with Tisha in the beginning? He couldn't remember, but he didn't think so. Tisha wasn't the type to wear such vulnerable emotions on her sleeve. Her approach was always guarded, as if she could never quite trust him completely. And now he was spending the day with another woman. Even though he had no plans to be anything more than friends with Ashleigh, he still knew Tisha wouldn't like him being there.

"Did you have any trouble finding the place?"

He stepped forward, shoving thoughts of Tisha to the background of his mind. "No, I followed the signs marked 'Serial killer hideout.' Seriously, Ash, could this place get any more remote?"

She smiled. "It's nice, isn't? Very secluded."

He allowed himself a mental eye roll at her forced oblivion. She obviously didn't want to talk about the danger she might be in, but it needed to be said. "Did anyone follow you this morning? Were there any suspicious cars around?"

Her smile turned sheepish. "To be honest, I don't know. I was sort of lost in my own little world, and the caffeine hadn't hit yet. I didn't start to wake up and pay attention until I arrived here."

Nick drew in a breath, held it, and let it out slowly. He had already learned it would do no good to lecture her over her safety. Telling Ashleigh something she didn't want to hear would be like talking to a brick wall. The woman took stubbornness to a whole new level. "What are you building here?" He glanced at the pieces of lumber behind her.

"A pantry," she said. "And a window seat. The owner had this house built, but he wants to add a few custom touches to give it some character. And I'm having a blast because he let me have carte blanche on the designs, so I'm getting to be as intricate as I want to be. I think he's going to like it."

He smiled again, enjoying her enthusiasm. It was possible his face was going to crack from all the smiling he had done the last few days, which was odd considering he was shot and in a lot of pain. But Ashleigh was fresh, innocent, and full of spirit. He couldn't not smile when he was with her. Being near her felt like applying spackling to some of the cracks in his soul. He groaned aloud, and Ashleigh took a step forward, resting her palm on her stomach.

"Nick, what is it? Are you in pain?"

"You're turning me into a sap, Ash," he said as he tucked a strand of hair behind her ear. Her hair was in a ponytail today, making her look even younger than Caleigh. She smiled up at him and his heart flipped.

"Nothing wrong with being a sap."

"Not in your world, maybe." Tension descended between them and lingered. Nick knew he should drop his hand from her face and take a step away, but he was immobilized, at least until someone spoke behind him.

"Hello."

Nick dropped his hand and whirled, automatically striking a defensive pose as he waited either to be attacked or attack, depending on the situation. But the man who faced him was small and harmless, albeit scared witless if the way he recoiled in fear was any indication. He actually put his arm up to block his face, as if he thought Nick was going to hit him for no reason. His over-the-top reaction made Nick wonder what his expression looked like, and he worked to subdue it. Good thing he no longer had all his facial piercings or the guy might run screaming into the woods.

"Mr. Baker, hello," Ashleigh said, easing forward with her arm outstretched. She laid her hand gently on his forearm and the soft touch had the desired effect of calming him. He blinked at her in confusion a few times, his glance darting warily to Nick and landing on his arm full of tattoos.

"Is this your assistant, Ashleigh? I was under the impression you worked alone."

"I do," Ashleigh replied. "Nick is a friend. Let me introduce you. Corporal Nick Lassiter, this is Mr. Henry Baker, soon to be Doctor Baker if all my pounding and hammering doesn't distract him from his thesis." She smiled at him and he smiled in return, almost squirming in delight at her words. Either the guy was really proud of his pending doctorate, or he was really into Ashleigh. Maybe both.

Nick stepped forward and held out his hand. The guy started to flinch before catching himself and forcing his hand out. "How do you do, sir? Congratulations on your doctorate. I barely finished my undergrad, I have no idea how people go for more."

The doctor relaxed and even managed a bit of smugness. "Yes, well, I'm not sure I would be very good at being a marine, Corporal."

Nick was fairly certain of that, too, but he didn't say it. The smaller man turned his attention to Ashleigh. "I was coming to tell you I'm going out for the rest of the day. Do you need anything?"

"No, thank you. I plan to work until about five. Will you be home then, or shall I lock up?"

"I'm not sure," he replied. "I suppose go ahead and lock up if I'm not here." He glanced at Nick, still wary despite his outward composure. "Will he be staying all day?"

Ashleigh looked at Nick, too. "Yes," Nick replied. No way was he leaving her here alone, and what else did he have to do besides lie on his stomach and not think about the pain in his butt?

"Okay, then," Mr. Baker said, though he made no move to leave. He glanced once more between Nick and his house, probably trying to calculate the odds Nick would pilfer the family silver, and then he left. Nick watched him go, his head tipped to the side as he studied the man. He was slightly older, probably mid-thirties, shorter, though it was difficult to say how short since Nick was taller than average. There was something off-putting about him, something more than his cowardice and suspicious nature. Nick continued his inspection as the man got in his car and buckled up, noting the fresh mud on his tires.

"Has he been here since you arrived today?" he asked Ashleigh. She had already returned to her work and had to pause and think about it.

"Yes. His car was in the drive when I pulled up."

"Hmm." He was alone in his suspicions because she was totally focused on what she was doing. "What are you doing?"

"Making joints. They'll hold the cabinet together."

"Isn't that what glue and nails are for?" he asked.

"If you want to do it the easy and cheap way, then yes. But joints are the benchmark of quality craftsmanship. Ideally you're creating connections that will stand the test of time and hold a piece of furniture together for hundreds of years. Now there are machines that make dovetailed joints, but a century ago people did it by hand. When you realize how much work and detail went into antiques, it makes them worth their price."

"If you say so," he said. He had never noticed such things as joints, quality, or craftsmanship. He was more into function. If a piece of furniture supported his weight and felt comfortable, then it was worthy of being in his house. Hearing her talk so lovingly about furniture was an enlightening experience because he had always wondered why people paid so much for furniture. Previously he had been under the impression it was snobbery on the part of the rich, but Ashleigh was far from rich. Perhaps there were other people in the world who had an appreciation for artistry.

"Do you want to own antiques or make your own?" he asked. He leaned against the side of her truck, taking the weight off his aching leg. The pain that had been concentrated to his behind was now radiating down his legs and up his back. Finding a comfortable position was becoming increasingly impossible.

"A combination, maybe. I want my house to be cozy and comfortable. If I buy antiques, they're going to be usable. I don't want to live in a museum. What about you? What does Nick's dream house look like?"

"I can honestly say no one has ever asked me that question before," Nick said, and he had no answer.

"Don't you ever dream about what you want your future to look like? The house, the wife, the kids, the car?"

"No, not once. Ever."

"Why not?"

She was planing something, he knew because she had showed him how to use the planer. He was momentarily distracted by watching her smooth the tool over the wood. There was something soothing about the repetitive motion that mesmerized him. "I don't know." Before he had said he was too young to think about such things, but she was five years younger. Maybe he didn't know what to plan for because he had no idea what he wanted, no idea what a settled future was supposed to look like.

"But you must have considered the possibility your future would involve becoming an officer," she said. "I mean, you got your degree for that purpose."

"I suppose," he said. "But I thought I would have more time. Now the moment has come, and I'm not sure I want to make the leap."

"I think you should, but I guess you already know that." She paused to hold up the board she was working on, tilting it toward the light to look for something he couldn't see. "Why did you become a marine?"

"Because I had nothing better to do."

She paused in her inspection, turning her steady gaze on him. "Why did you become a marine?"

How did she do that? How did she see so easily through his constructed façade? "Because of my father."

"I thought you said you didn't know who your father is."

"I don't, officially. When I was seventeen, I decided I wanted to find out. I asked my mother for a list of likely candidates and took a little road trip to the place where I was born. There was one guy I'm pretty sure is him. He looked like me, tall with hair and eyes the same color. It was like looking in a mirror in more ways than one."

"How so?"

"He was a loser. I knew before I met him he probably would be, but I think there's a little part of everyone that hopes their dad is secretly a superhero, you know? But then I saw him and knew for sure he was a loser. He worked odd jobs between getting raging drunk. He was in and out of jail. He was in the tank when I found him, tossed in for domestic violence, so I guess it's good my mom didn't stay with him. I went to see him, and I think he knew when he saw me I was his. The resemblance was unmistakable. To his credit, I guess he tried to give me what he thought was his philosophy on life. Never trust women. Never trust the police. Look out for number one. Do what you have to in order to get by. But it had the opposite effect of what he intended because I did the reverse of everything he suggested.

I had been on the fast track to distraction with too much alcohol and drugs. My run-ins with the cops were becoming more frequent, although thankfully my offenses were minor and didn't go on my record. But I could see it, I could see me turning into him, and it scared me. I called the recruiter the next day and never took another drug so my system would be clear by the time I took my screening evaluation."

"That's amazing," Ashleigh said. She had set down the piece of wood in order to give him her full attention.

"Which part, the possibility of several fathers, the real father who is now in prison, or the seventeen-year-old drug addict?"

"The kid who recognized the path he was heading and decided to change it with nothing to lean on but your own grit and determination. You have no idea how much I respect you."

Respect? Him? Had she not understood what he had told her? Did she not realize how different her pristine world was from his sullied one?

"What's your mother like?" she asked.

"My mother lives under the delusion it's the sixties and everywhere she goes is Woodstock. She's really into trying to find herself and at forty three she still hasn't managed to do it, despite years of searching. She uses her peace, love, and self-fulfillment philosophy as a cover for total self-absorption, though now the chickens are coming home to roost because years of heavy drug use are catching up with her and she's losing her mind."

She blinked at him, probably alarmed by his matter-of-fact tone, but he had cut emotional ties with his mother long ago. How could he continue to feel anything for a woman who constantly put her own needs and agenda above his? A woman who had dumped her four-year-old son on a stranger she met at the supermarket because she wanted to go to a rock concert in another state?

"I'm going to take this into the house," Ashleigh announced. Nick followed, feeling helpless while a woman who was a foot shorter carried several large pieces of lumber and he carried nothing. She didn't need his help and would probably chastise him for asking since he was injured, but that didn't mean he enjoyed the unsettling help-lessness.

"How did your team come together?" she asked.

"Kelsey and I met in basic. We were shipped to different units, but we had the shared goal of doing sniper school together. It wasn't easy to work because there are only a few openings per year and you have to meet a few other qualifications first. It was something of a miracle we made it in together and then made it through."

"Are Truck and Lolly snipers, too?"

"No. They've had training in reconnaissance, which is why they're on our team. It's not always about the shooting. Sometimes it's about gathering intelligence in a situation when other agencies might not be able to get in our out."

"What's the hardest part of your job?" she asked.

"The boredom." His answer was truthful and automatic, but then he paused, considering. Would she be put off by the fact that he hadn't said the killing? To an outsider, that would probably seem like the hardest part, but it wasn't. It was what he was trained for. Waiting for hours without end with few provisions was much harder.

"What kind of boredom? Mental or physical?"

"Both. There are times when I've had to remain in the exact same position for hours, sometimes days. I can't even twitch for fear of being discovered. Other times we're holed up in some house, waiting with nothing to do but stare at each other. And since we're already together all the time, there's not much left to discuss. This is where Kelsey is especially helpful because he can conjure conversation from nothing, like a magician. Of course it's usually the stupidest conversation ever, something you would never talk about in the real world."

Ashleigh was laughing, imagining what the irrepressible Kelsey might come up with. "Like what?"

"Once we spent fourteen hours arguing about what nuns wear under their habits. Lolly was especially disturbed by that one."

"What's Truck like? I couldn't get a read on him the other night."

"That's Truck for you. He plays his cards close to his chest, but he's a good guy. A little intense and angry sometimes, but when you're in the field, that's the kind of guy you want watching your back. He tends to personalize the job too much sometimes, though. He feels like the bad guys are out to get him, and he has the tendency to go a little overboard. I have to rein him in sometimes."

Ashleigh could picture it, the way they worked together. Kelsey was the clown, the one who kept things from being too heavy. Lolly was the nurturer. Truck was wary, watching over everything, and Nick was the leader, keeping his team on point, both physically and mentally. What she didn't understand was how he couldn't see what a natural leader he was. It was effortless. Some men would kill to have the character traits he had been born with—the charisma, wisdom, and ability to make snap decisions under pressure. He wasn't living up to his potential, and that made her sad.

The rest of the day was much the same with Ashleigh working and asking probing, intense questions. Nick had no idea why, but he answered them all with honesty. Maybe he was trying to scare her away, to show her how different his life was from hers, but she seemed to like him more with every question. And with every question, his chest felt a little lighter, as if he had secretly been longing to pour out his life story. He had never consciously felt that need, but now that it was happening he understood why some people went to therapy. It felt immensely good to talk, to try and puzzle out his past and the effect it had on his present.

The day ended, and there was no more reason to be with her, but he still didn't want to leave. She must have felt the same if the way she dawdled by her truck was any indication. "I guess I should go swap your car for my truck," he said. At least that would give him an excuse to go to her house, but she shook her head.

"Keep my car for the week. I'm afraid you'll tear your wound open if you keep getting in and out of your truck." She bit her lip and looked off into the trees while an awkward silence settled between them.

"Do you want to maybe come over and hang out for a while?" he asked. "I promise I won't make you cook or clean." He felt as shy and nervous as a kid asking for his first date, only when he'd had his first date he had been too young and stupid to be shy or nervous.

"I would like that," Ashleigh replied, sounding as timid as he felt. They remained, scuffling their feet in the gravel until Nick came to his senses and realized how stupid he looked. He cleared his throat and straightened.

"So I'll see you back at my place. Go first, and I'll follow."

"You know what's weird? When you tell me what to do, I actually want to obey," she said.

He helped her into her truck and closed the door. "Know what's even weirder? I feel the same way." He thumped the door of her truck and watched her drive away.

CHAPTER 13

Kelsey was asleep on the couch when Ashleigh and Nick entered his home. Nick felt a flash of guilt because he knew how hard the sergeant had been working his teammates as punishment for his absence. While he had spent the day in pleasant conversation with a pretty woman, his friends had no doubt slogged through a swamp in full gear.

Almost as soon as they stepped into the living room, the door opened, and Melly came in. She held out her hand to Ashleigh. "I don't think we formally met the other day. I'm Mellisandra, but everyone calls me Melly. I'm sorry I was rude and grumpy." She jerked her thumb to indicate Kelsey lying behind her. "He has that effect on me."

Ashleigh smiled and returned her handshake. "I'm Ashleigh. It's nice to meet you."

"Nice to meet you, too," Melly said. She reminded Ashleigh of Jesus —they both had kind eyes. Today her smile was open, friendly, and welcoming, at least until Kelsey reached up with both arms and pulled her down beside him on the couch. She yelped in surprise, her arms and legs flailing as she went down.

"It freaks me out when you do that whole sleep to wake thing with no in between," Melly said.

Kelsey enveloped her in his embrace, pressing his face to her neck. "Why do you think I do it?" he asked, his voice muffled. He reached down and flicked off her high heels, tossing them onto the floor. "How do you walk in these things?"

"Easily. It's standing all day that kills me."

"Don't wear them."

"It goes better for me if I'm taller than the kids I teach," she said. "It's hard to see someone as an authority figure if you're looking her in the eye."

"I see you as an authority figure, and I'm a foot taller," Kelsey said.

"Yes, but you're special."

His smile faded to a perplexed frown as he realized she hadn't meant that as a compliment. Ashleigh sat in the recliner and Nick stood beside her, leaning.

Melly nudged Kelsey. "Get up so Nick can sit down."

"No, it's okay," Nick said. "Standing is better."

"Yeah, standing is better," Kelsey agreed. He burrowed his face farther into Melly's neck. "Melly, why can't you be this cuddly all the time? You never let me hold you."

"My defenses are worn down today," she said. She sounded tired.

"Bad day, Luscious?" Kelsey murmured.

"Just long. What about you? What are you doing lying on the couch?"

"Tired. Less talking, more cuddling."

Melly rolled her eyes, but she didn't reply. Ashleigh watched them with a smile. She wasn't sure exactly what their relationship was. She didn't think they were dating, but neither were they like brother and sister. There was more than a flicker of attraction between them. She wondered if either one was aware of it.

"Nick and I were going to hang out, maybe get something to eat. Want to join us?" she asked.

"Sure," Melly agreed, but the word was cut short when Kelsey squeezed her waist, obviously trying to tell her he didn't want to. An awkward pall fell over the room. Kelsey realized he had been caught and tried to cover.

"You going to cook again, PK? Ashleigh cooks," he added, giving Melly another squeeze. "Unlike some women I know."

"Unlike all the women you know except me," she said, elbowing his ribs. "I cook. Not my fault if the wittle marine burned his tongue on a pepper."

"Uh, try my skin, my lips, my tongue, my esophagus, my stomach, my intestines, my…"

Melly covered his mouth with her hand. "We get it. You can't handle it hot. Some men can't. It's really okay."

He shook free of her hand. "I was having an off day. I had just come back from overseas, and I think I had a bug or something. I can handle hot food."

"Really, hotshot? You want a rematch?"

He glanced at Nick and Ashleigh in desperation. "I don't think you should make that kind of food for PK. It's probably a sin in her religion."

"I love hot food," Ashleigh said. "The hotter the better. If you're really up for it, we could make a little wager." She smiled, fluttering her lashes in an imitation of perfect innocence.

"That sounds awesome," Melly said. "Kelsey's always making bets with people. I'm sure he can probably take you, seeing as how he's such a stud muffin scout sniper, and all. There's not much he can't handle. Right, Jaws?" Now it was her turn to give him a sweet smile.

Kelsey looked at Nick. "What happened here?"

"I think the women have formed their own unit, and we're doomed," Nick said. "Good luck with the peppers."

Kelsey closed his eyes and groaned. His lids flapped open in surprise, however, when Melly put her arms around him. He leaned closer, returning her embrace until he realized she was simply pulling his wallet from his back pocket. "Hey!" He reached for it, but she dodged him and stood.

"You owe me, Adams."

"So you're going to light my insides on fire *and* you're going to make me pay for it."

"Pretty much," Melly said. She tucked his wallet into her purse and turned to Ashleigh. "Would you like to come to the store with me?"

"Sure," Ashleigh said.

"I'll come," Kelsey volunteered, but Melly shook her head.

"You stink like swamp water. Go shower."

He sniffed at himself and grimaced. "Oh, right. Shower. I knew there was something I forgot."

"Want me to come?" Nick offered, hoping they would say no. Besides the fact that his pain meds had worn off, he had no desire to tag along with two women who seemed intent on bonding.

"No, thanks," Ashleigh said. She reached up, resting her hand on his bicep. "Maybe you should lie down for a bit. You look all done in."

"Pfft." Everyone turned to look at Kelsey who didn't say anything beyond the incredulous noise.

"Maybe I will," Nick agreed, causing Kelsey to sigh.

"C'mon, Ashleigh," Melly said. "Let's go before Kelsey's leak gets any worse. *What is wrong with you?*" She mouthed the last part to him and shook her head. "I'm sorry about that, about him," she said as soon as she and Ashleigh stepped outside.

"It's okay. He already told me he doesn't like me," Ashleigh said. "Good thing for me I'm not one of those people who needs constant approval."

"He'll come around," Melly said. "He doesn't do well with change."

"Did he have this same sort of trouble with Tisha?"

"Well, no, but Tisha's different."

"How so?" Ashleigh asked. Melly's car was behind hers, so she slid in the passenger seat and buckled her safety belt.

"Tisha is temporary," Melly said.

"But I thought she and Nick have been dating a long time."

"Yes and no. They've been together for a long time in measures of quantity, but for much of that time the guys have been out of the country. I don't think their relationship has consisted of much quality time. I think if they ever really spent a lot of time together they would break up." She paused and bit her lip, shooting Ashleigh a look before she backed out. "Can I ask what's up with you and Nick? Take this as a compliment when I tell you you're not his usual type."

"I wish I had an answer for that question, but I really don't know. I mean, I think we're trying to be friends, but there's this thing between us. Have you ever been completely attracted to someone despite the fact that you really shouldn't be?"

"Oh, yeah," Melly said, giving her head an emphatic nod.

"Kelsey?"

Melly chuckled. "Uh, no. I'm stupid, but I'm not that stupid, at least not anymore. Don't get me wrong, Kelsey is the most beautiful man I've ever seen. I mean, seriously, if the body doesn't get you, the eyes and face will. But he's like one of those tropical birds who sits and stares at itself in a mirror all day, admiring its plumage." She shook her head. "I love him. Besides my brother, he's my best friend. But I wouldn't be so cruel as to inflict him on me. He's perpetually fifteen and totally shallow. No way."

Methinks thou dost protest too much, Ashleigh thought, but she wisely remained silent. They were both a little relieved when they arrived at the store and the topic of Nick and Kelsey came to a close. Ashleigh stood back and watched in awe as Melly chose ingredients Ashleigh had never heard of before.

"People actually use tomatillos?" she asked.

"Mexican people do," Melly assured her.

"Did you grow up in Mexico?"

"No. My parents were from a small town outside Mexico City. I was born over the border and grew up in California. My mom cooked pure Mex, but I was influenced by the Baja region."

"I have no idea what that means," Ashleigh said. "I've never been west of Ohio."

"Baja is a little lighter, it uses fresher ingredients and less lard."

Ashleigh wrinkled her nose. "People still use lard?"

"Yes, a lot. I'm going to use some in the tortillas."

"You're going to make your tortillas?" Ashleigh realized she was sounding like a broken record with so many questions. She shook her head. "You're like some kind of culinary wizard, Melly. I'm surprised the guys don't beg you to cook for them every night."

"They would, if I let them. I decided long ago I didn't want to be their den mother, you know? It would be their ultimate dream come true if I came every day, cooked for them, cleaned up, and did their laundry. I keep Jesus well fed, but the others aren't my responsibility. Truck and Whit aren't so bad, but Kelsey is a taker. I have no patience for his manipulation, but Jesus is a softer touch. More often than not, Kelsey convinces him to take him along to my house for supper so I end up feeding both of them. I draw the line at his girlfriends, though."

"Has he tried to bring dates to your house?" Ashleigh asked.

"Only once."

"What did you do?"

"I pretended I didn't speak English and refused to let them in. His girlfriend threatened to call immigration on me. They got into a big fight and broke up, right there on my lawn." She chuckled. "It was awesome."

"Melly, I think you and I are going to get along really well," Ashleigh said.

"I would like that," Melly said, sobering. "I don't really have any female friends. I keep saying it's because I'm new, but I've lived here three years. I have acquaintances at work, but they're all so busy with their own lives."

"I don't really have any friends and I've lived here my whole life," Ashleigh said. "Women don't tend to like me because I don't temper my words."

"I like straightforward people. You always know where you stand." They smiled at each other.

"Are you and Tisha good friends?" Ashleigh asked.

"No, we're not any kind of friends. Tisha is territorial and antisocial. In the beginning I tried to make her understand I had no interest in Nick, but now we simply choose to ignore each other. It would be nice if he dated someone I could actually be friends with."

"I don't think that's a likely scenario," Ashleigh said. "But we can still be friends. I would like that."

When they arrived back at the house, Nick had taken Kelsey's place on the couch and Kelsey was sitting in the recliner, ESPN blaring on the television. He held out his hand for his wallet, and Melly placed it in his palm as she passed. Ashleigh used the opportunity to pause beside Nick and admire his sleeping form. He was so cute when he slept. And when he was awake. Before she met him, she never would have believed a marine could be so endearing.

Melly oversaw the supper preparations, assigning tasks to Ashleigh like her mother had done when she was a little girl. She didn't mind because she had no idea what she was doing. Mexican cuisine was unfamiliar to her.

"Maybe you can teach me to cook southern, and I could teach you to cook Mex," Melly suggested.

"I would like that," Ashleigh said. "Would you like me to make some sweet tea?"

Melly tried hard not to wrinkle her nose. "If you'd like. I haven't yet developed a taste for the stuff, but I know the guys like it."

Ashleigh set about her task, relieved to be doing something familiar, and then the food was ready. The spicy smell was making her mouth water.

"It even smells hot," Kelsey said as he made his way into the kitchen, lured by the scent. Nick wasn't far behind, though he only looked half awake. Ashleigh took a step toward him before she realized she had been about to slip her arms around his waist. That was a definite no-no.

"How are you feeling?" she asked instead.

"Fine," he said.

"I'm learning that word has all kinds of meanings when you use it," she said. She spotted the aspirin sitting beside the fridge and shook two into his palm before pouring him a glass of iced tea to wash them down. When she turned toward the table, Kelsey was studying her with a sullen expression. Melly noticed, too, and jabbed him in the side.

He winced and moved out of her reach. "What was that for?"

"You know," she said, her tone cryptic.

"You have freakishly bony fingers," he accused.

"Good comeback," she said, and Nick and Ashleigh laughed. Nick held Ashleigh's chair for her. She flushed with pleasure, sure it wasn't something he often remembered to do.

"So what's the wager?" Nick asked.

"Et tu, bro?" Kelsey said.

"I want to see how hot the food has to be to make you cry," Nick said.

"I don't cry," Kelsey said. "I sweat through my eyes. And it's not going to happen tonight. Let's do this." He turned to Ashleigh. "You're going down, PK."

"Bring it," Ashleigh said.

"Tough talk from a little girl," he said.

"Fine. Let's stop talking and do this thing." She dished up a hefty serving of the enchiladas and mole, one for herself, one for him, and then decided to serve Melly and Nick while she was at it and had the spoon in her hand. Melly pulled out the bowl of chopped raw peppers, sprinkling an equal amount over Ashleigh and Kelsey's plates.

"Ready?" Ashleigh asked when Melly finished. "First one to take a drink or use sour cream as medicine loses. Count it off, Nick."

They stared at Nick as he raised his fork in the air. "Three, two, one, eat." Nick and Melly picked at their food while Ashleigh and Kelsey began shoveling enchiladas into their mouths. After the fourth bite, Kelsey sputtered to a stop.

"Hold up. I don't trust you women. How do I know there wasn't some prearranged deal where I get the ghost peppers and PK gets nothing?"

Without a word, Ashleigh switched her plate for his and continued eating. Kelsey repressed a sigh and reluctantly returned to his plate. Kelsey's bites became slower and his chewing sessions longer while Ashleigh showed no signs of slowing down. She cleaned her plate while he still had half to go.

"You gave me more," he complained. She added another scoop of enchiladas to her plate, along with another heaping teaspoon of chopped peppers.

"I think your eyes are beginning to sweat," she said.

He took one more bite before tossing his fork onto his plate and dashing for the sink, eyes streaming. "This is possibly the best moment of my life," Melly said.

"That was awesome," Nick agreed. He leaned over and put his arms around Ashleigh, giving her an impromptu hug.

In all the excitement, no one had heard Tisha enter until she spoke. "Well, this looks cozy."

ick let Ashleigh go and sat back. "Tish, what are you doing here?"

She frowned at his less-than-enthusiastic greeting. "Kelsey called me and told me to come over."

All eyes swiveled to Kelsey who appeared to be trying to drown himself with the faucet. "I bod she should be dere," he said as he held out his tongue, dousing it with cold water. He noticed Melly's glare and angled himself away.

Ashleigh wasn't usually at a loss for words, but as she watched Tisha and Nick stare at each other, she was. What was she doing here? She wasn't the woman who horned in on another woman's territory. True, she and Nick technically hadn't kissed since that first time, since before she knew he was attached. But there were undercurrents simmering between them they were nurturing by being together. All of a sudden she felt guilty, especially in light of the hurt and misery on the other woman's face. What should she do to make things better? Apologize?

Melly, noting the stricken look on Ashleigh's face, intervened. "Would you like something to eat, Tisha? It's a little hot, though. Too hot for some." She darted another furious glance at Kelsey who had stopped dousing his tongue but still didn't return to the table. *Coward,* she thought.

"No, thanks, I'm not hungry," Tisha said.

The combination of anger and dismay in her tone made Ashleigh's stomach roil with regret. She had hurt this person by her careless disregard, and she was sorry. Tears pricked the backs of her eyes, closing her throat. Fleeing seemed the only answer, so she shot to her feet. "I should go."

Nick tipped his face up at her, his lips twisting into a frown as he noted her expression and the tears shimmering unshed on her lashes. The fact that he seemed more upset over her emotional display than Tisha's wasn't helping matters, and she had to get out before things could get worse.

"Thanks for supper, Melly," she said, her voice breaking on the last word. She sprinted from the house, accidentally slamming the front door in her haste to get away.

The silence left in the kitchen was oppressive.

"What," Tisha began, but Nick interrupted.

"Let's take it outside," he said. He stood and ushered her outside, practically shoving her resistant body to get her there. Melly thought it a wise thing to do because Tisha tended to throw and break things when she was angry.

"Think she'll hit him?" Kelsey asked.

Melly tore her eyes from the back door and rested them on him. He was smiling, the dope. "What did you do?"

His smile slipped at her angry tone. "I thought his girlfriend should know what's going on. If we're having family bonding time, don't you think it's right she be here?"

Melly stood and began angrily clearing dishes from the table.

"What? Melly, why are you so mad?" Kelsey pressed.

"You embarrassed Ashleigh," Melly said.

"So? What is she to us? We've known her less than a week. Who cares if she's embarrassed?"

The dishes clattered into the sink as Melly spun on him. "Anyone with a heart should care. Ashleigh is a nice person who doesn't deserve what you did to her."

"Nice people don't make men cheat on their girlfriends. Or didn't you think of that? Shouldn't our loyalty be to Tisha here?"

"Is that what this is about?" Melly said. "Did you do this for Tisha?"

He didn't reply. Instead he carried a stack of plates to the sink and began to scrape them clean.

"You want to know why I'm so mad, Kelsey? I'll tell you. It's because I know you, and I know this has nothing to do with Ashleigh or Tisha or even Nick. It's all about you; it always is."

"So?" he said, turning to stare at her with a defiant look on his too-handsome face. "Why should things have to change because Nick meets someone new? Things are good as they are."

"For you, maybe."

"You don't think he's happy with Tisha? She's his usual type, and they've been together for a year. That's longer than he's been with anybody."

"No, I don't think he's happy with Tisha," Melly said. "I think he's settling for Tisha because he feels like she's all that's out there. But Ashleigh is opening his eyes to a different type of woman, one who could actually be his partner in life, one who could make things better instead of being dependent on him for her emotional wellbeing. He has a real chance at happiness here, and you're trying to take that away because everything is all about you, isn't it, Kelsey?"

"So what if it is?" Kelsey said, finally provoked to anger by her words. She was confusing him, making him think maybe he hadn't done the right thing. He had thought he was looking out for Nick by trying to keep the status quo the same, but if what Melly had said was true, then maybe he was actually harming Nick in the long run. "If it's not about me, then what's the point? Why should I care?"

Truck and Lolly entered the house and poked their heads into the kitchen, alerted by the sound of yelling and the smell of food. Lolly saw the remnants of his sister's cooking on the table and sat down, picking up a fork as he dug in. Truck sat beside him, observing the latest round of Melly v. Kelsey.

For a long time, Melly looked at him as if plumbing the depths of his soul, trying to find some elusive quality. Kelsey resisted the urge to squirm under her inspection. At last she took a breath and shook her head. He thought maybe her anger had spent itself, but he was wrong because when she opened her mouth, it was to emit a rapid stream of Spanish. He couldn't understand a word she said, but the tone was pretty clear.

She finished saying whatever it was and stomped out of the house, not even pausing to say hello to her little brother.

Kelsey felt a mixture of pain and regret that made him angry because he couldn't understand it. "Someday I'm going to learn Spanish, and then you'll be sorry," he yelled, even thought Melly was already gone.

"I know Spanish, and you should be sorry now, Bro," Lolly said. "What did you do?"

"Why do you always assume it was me? Maybe Melly did something," Kelsey said. Truck and Lolly stared at him until he turned away from them in disgust. "PK was here, and I invited Tisha over. It, uh, didn't go well. Tisha and Nick are outside now."

"Good," Truck said. "Better the enemy you know than the enemy you don't. I don't trust that Ashleigh girl. No one is that nice. She must be hiding something."

"She's hiding the fact that her ex, a marine, beat her and threatened her," Lolly said, sounding as angry and exasperated as his sister had. "Jaws, why would you do that? Don't you understand Ashleigh could be good for Nick?"

"No, I don't," Kelsey said. "What's the big deal? Women are women. How much effect can one have on a man?"

"Amen," Truck said.

"You guys are hopeless," Lolly said.

"Says the priest who's never had a woman," Truck said.

"When I do, she'll be something special," Lolly said. "I won't have to write her name on a piece of paper so I remember what it is in the morning." He and Truck looked at Kelsey.

"That happened one time," Kelsey said. "And I was drunk."

"Yes because that makes it so much better," Lolly said.

"Why don't you go for Ashleigh?" Kelsey suggested. "You like her so much, you take her."

"If I thought she would have me, then I would. But she's Nick's, and he's hers, even if you don't see that yet. I don't get why you can't understand the difference between the women you bring home and women like Ashleigh and Melly."

Kelsey shifted and turned away at the mention of Melly. She *was* different than other women, though he wasn't sure how. Maybe because he knew her and there had never been romance between them. She was like family, and he didn't like to associate her with the string of casual romantic encounters he tried to pass off as relationships. Was that how Nick saw Ashleigh, as something special, as being different from the others? Still, why did it have to change everything? Kelsey wasn't ready for change, and he felt Nick shouldn't be, either. Twenty seven was too young for commitment, and Ashleigh had *commitment* written all over her.

He filled the sink with soapy water. He couldn't remember the last time he had washed dishes, but if Melly came back and the mess wasn't cleaned up, it would be another strike against him. If she only knew the ways he pushed himself to be better for her, she wouldn't be so hard on him, he thought. He worked up a good pout, feeling very sorry for himself as he stared out the window and wondered how Nick was faring with Tisha.

Not well, would have been Nick's reply if he knew what his best friend was thinking. Tisha was quiet, which had never happened before. Screaming tantrums he could handle, but her pained silence was killing him.

"So, what, you're blatantly cheating on me now?" she asked at last. He could tell she was trying to hold on to her anger, but too much hurt was leaking through.

"No, Tish, it's not like that with her. I told you."

"So you've never touched her," she pressed.

He could have lied to her. He had lied often in the past to avoid an emotional outburst, but he was suddenly tired of the being the person he had been. "Once, in the hospital. She kissed me, but she didn't know I had a girlfriend. There hasn't been anything since then."

Tisha snorted. "Right, Nick. I'm supposed to believe you've been with her and not touched her. She's pretty." She flung out the last word as an accusation.

"I'm telling you she's not like that. She's a virgin."

Tisha laughed then. It was supposed to be a derisive, mocking laugh, but it sounded more heartbroken than amused. "A virgin. Great. How am I supposed to compete with that?"

"It's not a competition," Nick said.

"Isn't it? Because from where I stand, it is. You like this person, I can tell." She swallowed hard, and Nick winced. Tisha was far more comfortable using anger than tears. If she was crying, then she was truly hurt, and he felt horrible about that. They hadn't always had the best relationship, but he didn't want to hurt her.

"I'm sorry," he said, pouring all the sincerity he felt into the words. "I'm really sorry, Tish. I never intended to hurt you. And I wasn't trying to cheat on you with Ashleigh, I swear. This whole thing has come out of nowhere, and I'm a little off-kilter myself." He drew in a breath, held it, and let it out slowly. "Maybe we should take a little break and think about some things."

"Are you breaking up with me?" she asked.

"No, I...I'm confused. I need some space and time to think, and I think you should do that, too."

"What's there to think about?" Tisha said, some of her old anger returning. "Either you want to be with me, or you don't. And if you think I'm going to sit on my hands and wait for you to make up your mind, you're mistaken. It's over, Nick. Forget you. Forget everything."

Her anger was spiraling out of control. He braced himself, waiting for her to hit him, but she didn't. Instead she turned her rage on the grill, grabbing it with both hands and pulling it over so hard it bounced a couple of times. She circumvented the house by walking through the yard. A minute later, he heard her car pull away.

He sat outside for a long time, staring at the upended grill, trying to feel a sliver of grief over the end of his relationship with Tisha. He was sorry he had hurt her, but he felt no sadness at her loss. Instead, there was a whole lot of relief and something that felt like hope. Maybe he didn't have to be with a woman whose anger was so destructive she tore down everything she touched. Maybe he could be with a woman whose heart was whole and intact, someone like Ashleigh. From there his mind took the next logical step. Why not Ashleigh? What was to stop them from trying to make a go of things? They liked each other, they were attracted to each other, and they were both available now.

For a moment, his elation was so great he wanted to hop in the car, drive to her house, and beg her to give them a chance. But the longer he sat outside staring at the grill, the more his hope dimmed. Ashleigh had everything to offer him, but what did he have to offer in return? He was a corporal who shared a rental house with three other men. The only thing he owned outright was his ghillie suit. His truck cost a steep monthly payment, and it wasn't even that nice. He couldn't go to Ashleigh and expect her to accept him as he was. His intentions were good where she was concerned, but he had never managed to be the stable boyfriend, as proved by the fact that he had basically cheated on Tisha with Ashleigh.

And what of his life in the corps? Lots of women had a rosy view of military life until they experienced it. He had seen countless coworkers divorce over the long deployments and separations. He was luckier than some because he wasn't stationed with a battalion—Camp LeJeune was his home for the foreseeable future. But he was sent out on assignment every few weeks, sometimes for long stretches with no set end date. The job ended when it was completed, and that often depended on variable factors. Could he subject Ashleigh to that lifestyle? She who was so stable and dependable. Would she be able to cope with being with someone who was only around part time?

Then he realized the extreme path his thoughts had taken and experienced instant recoil. He was picturing forever, and he had only known her a week. What was wrong with him? He had kissed her once and spent a few hours talking, and he was suddenly ready for infinity. The old familiar panic gripped his soul and held on tight. He wasn't ready for forever with anyone, not even Ashleigh. Especially not Ashleigh. What did he know about being with a good girl? He only knew women like Tisha. What did Ashleigh do when she was angry? Did she internalize it? Verbalize it? How was he supposed to handle the church thing? And her family? He had never been with a woman who had a relationship with her family. They would no doubt be involved in everything, overseeing his every move to make sure he didn't hurt their daughter. Was he ready for that? He pictured Reverend Desmond's stern face and shuddered. No, he definitely wasn't ready for that.

His thoughts swirled round and round, overriding the pain in his backside from sitting so long in one position. He stayed on the back patio until late, until all his roommates had gone to bed, and when he finally went to sleep he still had no answers.

CHAPTER 15

The morning brought clarity. Nick needed space, not only from Tisha, but from Ashleigh. Kelsey's fears about Ashleigh had rubbed off, making Nick feel like he was in danger of losing himself if he continued down his current path. Was she really worth giving up everything? For twenty seven years, he had lived a carefree life, answering to no one, taking care of no one but his teammates. Why should any of that change for one woman?

Though he didn't exactly feel happy and carefree as he sat on the rubber doughnut, brooding over a cup of coffee. In fact, he felt a little empty as he imagined Ashleigh waking up at the crack of dawn, driving to the remote location with only the obnoxious Henry Baker as company. Would she notice his absence? Would she take it for what it was—a rebuff? He didn't want to hurt her; he simply wanted to protect himself and his way of life.

His teammates rose and left for work, wearily dragging on their gear for what was undoubtedly going to be another day of hard training. Kelsey avoided both eye contact and conversation, which was good since Nick wasn't sure if he was angry with him. Would he have done the same thing if he thought Kelsey was falling too hard and too fast for some woman? Since it had never happened before, he didn't know. With the exception of Melly, no woman ever stuck around long enough to sink her claws into Kelsey's well-preserved heart. Maybe he was right and that was the way to go because Kelsey had certainly never sat at the kitchen table, staring at a mug of coffee as it grew tepid while his heart flipped and squeezed in his chest. What was wrong with him? Why this woman? Why now? Why couldn't Ashleigh have come along ten years from now when he had sewed all his oats and was ready to settle down? Surely by then he would be ready for everything she represented—marriage, family, commitment, and being a real grownup.

His sullen introspection was interrupted by the jangling of his phone. He had left it on the counter, so it was with effort he heaved himself up and hobbled across the room. He almost didn't answer because it was his sergeant, but being a marine didn't allow for dodging calls from his boss. He was on call anytime, anywhere; even when he was on leave he wasn't really out of reach. Emergencies that required him circumvented anything in his personal life—it was the price he paid for possessing certain skills no one else did.

"Sir," Nick answered.

"How's your butt, corporal?"

"Uh, fine, Sergeant."

"No, I mean I really need to know. Are you functional?"

"I can be."

"Good, because the situation you were supposed to take care of has been turned from a simmer to a boil and we need you. You're going to go to the doctor today and if he gives you the all clear, then you're going wheels up tomorrow."

"Yes, Sergeant," Nick said. He kept his voice to a bored monotone, but inside he was elated. Not only would his forced vacation be over, but he would have a legitimate reason to avoid Ashleigh.

"The doc has me on speed dial. You'll be briefed after I get the all clear. Your team has been dismissed for some liberty before you fly."

This was the Sergeant's way of saying Nick was forgiven for the idiocy of being shot in Starbucks. "Thank you, sir." As he finished the words, the front door opened and the rest of his team trooped in, bringing renewed energy and optimism with them. Spirits were always high before a mission as adrenaline began snaking its way slowly through their veins, but after such a grueling couple of days, the guys were practically flying with news of their reprieve.

"Don't thank me yet, Corporal. The doctor gives you a no-go, and I swear I'll make you sorry you were ever born."

"Yes, Sergeant," Nick said. His sergeant had no toleration for weakness, but only because he possessed none himself. The man was a machine, but buried somewhere beneath all the metal was a heart that occasionally flickered. Nick and the others might grumble at his rough treatment, but deep down they had nothing but respect for the man. He was an old-school marine, born before political correctness or men found their feminine sides. His retirement was looming closer and closer and would bring a sad loss for the corps.

"Hey, Man," Truck, followed by Lolly, streamed their way into the kitchen. Kelsey was obviously still in avoidance mode, or maybe he was tired because he bypassed the kitchen and went to his room.

"Hey," Nick said.

"So our mission is resting on your butt. Literally," Truck said.

"No pressure," Lolly added.

"I think I'll pass inspection," Nick said, feigning more confidence than he felt. If the doctor had any idea how much pain he was in, there was no way he'd let him go.

"I can take you," Lolly volunteered.

"That's not necessary," Nick said.

"No, but it's better. I'll do it."

Lolly was an interesting little marine. Nick and Kelsey might be the snipers, but of all of them, Lolly was the most lethal. Nick and Kelsey used rifles; Lolly used his hands. He was one of those marines who would be a danger to society if he ever went crazy because he was a precise killing machine with the ability to disappear completely. So while the others might joke with him about his tender heart and almost girlish sensibilities, the teasing never went too deep. They might not understand him, but they respected him, both for what he was capable of and who he was. Nick especially didn't understand him. While he had undergone desensitization in sniper school by watching video after video of people being slaughtered, Lolly had no such training. He seemed both desensitized to killing and appalled by it. His religion didn't believe in murder, yet Lolly had killed more men than any of them. Nick didn't understand how those two concepts went together in the little marine's head, but somehow they did because he was saner than the rest of them, and more at peace, too.

"All right," Nick agreed though, with Lolly, one didn't so much give permission as come around of his way of thinking. He was like Ashleigh in that regard—when he believed he was doing the right thing, there was no changing his mind. Thoughts of Ashleigh brought a stab of pain and guilt, and so he pushed them away. Lolly poured his coffee into a travel mug, and they walked out together.

"So you and Tish are finished," Lolly said.

"Tish and I are finished," Nick confirmed.

"How are you doing with that?"

Nick sighed. Since his first day on the team, Lolly had elected himself as their very own Jiminy Cricket, keeping close tabs on the inner workings of their souls. "Fine, Lolly. Just fine."

Lolly nodded. "And Ashleigh, how did she take it when you told her?"

"I haven't told her."

"Why not?" Lolly asked. "If it were me, I would have driven over there last night as soon as Tisha left."

"You're not me," Nick said, sharper than he had intended, which made him feel immediately guilty. The thing about Lolly was that no matter how much you might want to be irritated at him for his intrusion into personal matters, it was impossible. He was a tagalong kid brother to all of them, and they loved him with equal devotion. Not to mention they would have to face Melly's wrath if they ever hurt her kid brother's feelings. Kelsey might enjoy the challenge of facing her down, but Nick found her terrifying when she was in a rage. Not that she had ever been angry with him or Truck. No, she saved all her poisonous darts for Kelsey who was especially good at provoking them.

"It's complex, Lolly," Nick added, softening his tone. What would Lolly know about matters of the heart? He had never even had a girlfriend.

"What's complex? You like Ashleigh; I can tell."

"I do, but she's not…we're not compatible."

"Why not?"

"Because she's good," Nick said.

"So are you," Lolly said.

Nick chuckled and shook his head over Lolly's devotion. He almost hated to enlighten him. "No, kid, I'm not."

"Whit, you've been my team leader for three years. Do you really think I don't know you? I've listened to every wild story you have. But I'm not talking about the things you've done. I'm talking about who you are; I'm talking about what's in your heart."

Nick stared out the window, disconcerted by Lolly's words. Where was Kelsey with an inappropriate yet mood-lightening joke when he needed him? "I don't want to talk about it." Great, now he sounded sullen. With relief, they pulled into one of the medical clinics at the naval hospital. Lolly remained wisely silent while Nick registered and waited his turn in the lobby. When the nurse called his name, he had never been so happy to be led to an exam room before.

"Good morning, Corporal." The nurse spoke in the no-nonsense chipper tone nurses everywhere seemed to possess, military or not.

"Ma'am," Nick replied. He sat perched on the edge of the table, trying not to wince as his backside made contact. The nurse stuck a thermometer in his mouth. What did his temperature have to do with being shot in the behind? He didn't ask, both because he couldn't talk and because the nurse outranked him. She took his blood pressure, made some notes on his chart, and left the room.

A short time later the doctor entered. "Corporal."

"Sir," Nick said. He sprawled on his stomach so the doctor could examine his wound. Despite the fact that he was basically naked from the waist down, he had never been more relieved to lie on his belly. The pain had moved from a deep muscle ache to a stinging skin wound. He hoped that was a good sign.

"How are you doing, Corporal?"

"Well, sir," Nick responded.

"How is your pain?"

"It's fine, sir. Manageable."

"You taking a prescription?" The doctor's voice tightened as if he thought Nick might be on heavy narcotics.

"No, sir. Over the counter stuff."

"Hmm." He leaned in, looked at the wound, and poked. Whether it was a natural action or a test, Nick didn't know. Either way, he didn't allow himself to react to the sharp stab of pain. "I'm not privy to your assignment, Corporal. Will you be digging ditches, doing any sort of heavy construction?"

"No, sir. There will probably be a lot of lying around like this." Of course that part would only come after they had to cross through enemy territory to get there and then would probably include an all-out sprint as they got out before they were noticed.

"Hmm," the doctor said again. "No sign of infection. The sutures are healing nicely. I'm going to give you an antibiotic, and I want you to take it with you. Who knows what kind of dirt and bacteria you'll be exposed to over there? I also want you to take along some antibacterial wipes and clean the wound twice a day. I know how you jarheads are about that sort of thing, Corporal, but that's the deal breaker. Give me your word you'll take the meds, keep it clean, and do your best to take it easy."

"Yes, sir," Nick replied, infusing his voice with all the earnestness he could muster. If the doctor wanted him to throw on a tutu and dance the Fandango, then he would agree to it so long as it meant he was cleared for duty.

"Then I reluctantly give you my clearance. You're not dying, and it's not worth the pressure I'm receiving to keep you here. Do what I said, okay?"

"Yes, sir," Nick agreed again, with enthusiasm this time.

The doctor shook his head. "Marines," he muttered. He wrote on a script pad, tore it off, and handed it to Nick before letting himself out the door.

"Sailors," Nick muttered, giving the door a hard look. Navy and marine personnel had a not-so-secret rivalry, even though the two branches often went hand in glove.

Lolly looked up when Nick entered the lobby, unable to mask the hopeful look in his too-expressive eyes. Nick gave him a heads-up nod, and Lolly pumped his fist in the air. "When do we go?" Lolly asked.

"Tomorrow."

"Are you going to call Ashleigh?"

Nick gave him a look, one he usually reserved for when they were on duty and needed to pull rank.

"I guess I'll call Melly," Lolly said, quickly changing the subject. Nick eavesdropped as he called his sister and told her he would be leaving in the morning. "No, I don't want to go out. Come over. Melly, no, I'm not your go-between. Suck it up and come over." He rolled his eyes as he set down his phone. "You think Melly and Jaws will ever get it together?"

Nick shrugged, but he was happy to have the focus off himself and his too complicated love life. "I dunno. I mean, they're kind of an odd mix, don't you think? Jaws is, well, Jaws. And Melly's so pristine."

"Yeah," Lolly said, staring off into the distance as if deep in thought. "Sometimes I wish I could direct everybody's life in the way I want it to go."

"Including yours?" Nick asked.

"Mine's going okay." He paused giving it more thought. "I wouldn't mind having a girl, though." He grinned up at Nick and Nick gave his shoulder a shove. Kelsey could make him laugh, but it was Lolly who truly made him feel lighter inside, as if maybe the world wasn't as dark as he thought it was. Curiously, he got the same feeling when he was with Ashleigh. He wondered why that was.

They arrived home and Nick went to his room, presumably to pack, but really he was going to take a nap. He was zonked, and who knew when he would be able to sleep in a real bed again? Or sleep at all for that matter. It had become a necessity to be able to sleep anywhere at any time, but that type of sleep wasn't as restful as actually lying down in a comfortable bed not inside an active combat zone.

Two hours later, he woke and threw his bag together. After so many years in the military, packing was a routine he didn't have to dither over. He knew exactly what to take, down to the smallest detail, and he never forgot anything because, in the field, the smallest thing could mean the difference between comfort and misery.

Kelsey was in the living room, having commandeered his usual spot in front of ESPN. Truck lay sprawled on the couch, meaning Melly and Lolly were probably in his room. It was a mystery what they did in there for hours at a time, but it must have included heavy conversation because occasionally Melly came away with red eyes, as if she had been crying. No one commented on it because Melly wasn't a crier and the only one close enough to ask her about it was Kelsey. But Kelsey was also either afraid to broach the subject or oblivious to any problems on Melly's part.

Now that Nick thought about it, he found it odd Lolly never mentioned anything about his sister. Over three years of countless hours spent together, they had bared their souls about many aspects. Melly had never come up.

He picked up his phone and checked for any messages, but there were none. His disappointment was unwarranted, especially because if Ashleigh had called he would have felt stifled. As it was, he simply felt guilty. He should call her. He should explain why he hadn't showed up today—because he was a coward—and tell her he was leaving the country for an unspecified amount of time. But the more he thought about it, the more he talked himself out of the idea. She wasn't his girlfriend. He barely knew her. He didn't owe her anything, least of all an explanation. The annoying ache in his chest was a reaction to being shot and breaking up with Tisha.

The door to Lolly's room opened and Melly stepped out. She passed through the living room without a word. Kelsey gave no indication he saw or heard her until she was directly behind his chair. Then his hand shot out, grabbing her wrist as he tugged her around the chair and into his lap.

"We're leaving the country. You have to make up with me; it's the law," he said.

They stared each other down, considering. "Bring me my brother unscathed, and I'll consider forgiving you," Melly said.

"Say something nice to me and it's a deal," Kelsey replied.

"You're freakishly handsome," Melly said.

"I already knew that, and you used that one last time. Say something else, something about my hidden depth as a person, junk like that."

"You know I don't believe in lying," Melly said. She squealed in laughter and tried to squirm away when Kelsey leaned forward and bit her neck.

Nick bestowed a benevolent smile on the scene now so familiar it was almost a rite of passage before any mission. No matter what Kelsey and Melly were arguing about, they always made up before he went away. Nick breathed in and out, a sigh of contentment. Things were getting back to normal. All he had to do was get back to work, and he would forget Ashleigh Desmond entirely. He was almost sure of it.

CHAPTER 16

"I'm bored. Amuse me, monkey." Kelsey clapped his hands in Lolly's direction. Lolly gave him a scathing look, but otherwise didn't reply.

"Dude, why do we go through this on every mission?" Truck asked. "Why did you become a scout sniper if you don't like the waiting?"

"Nobody told me there would be waiting. I thought it would be all, 'Blam, you're dead, compliments of the U.S. Marines. Have a nice day.' Instead we're all, 'Wait, watch, wait, watch, wait, watch.' Driving me crazy."

Nick could have pointed out they had been told over and over about the waiting, but he knew Kelsey wasn't being serious. He had gone into training with his eyes wide open, eyes that had been opened even more after weeks of training that bordered on torture. In fact, they had been tortured—water boarded, to be exact. That part had been the worst for him, the near breaking point, but it was Kelsey who talked him through, who pressed him not to quit.

That's never going to happen in the real world, Kelsey promised. *Get through it here, and we'll make* sure *it never happens again.* Nick had understood what he meant. They would never let it get to that point on assignment by either neutralizing their targets or neutralizing each other.

Kelsey talked a big game about being bored or scared or pushed beyond his limit, but Nick knew it was all mindless bluster. In reality, there was nothing that bothered Kelsey, nothing he couldn't shrug off and forget. Their friendship was the only lasting thing in his life, and it, too, was on precarious ground right now. They still hadn't talked over the Ashleigh/Tisha situation, and the tension was palpable. Lolly had tried to force a conversation on the plane over the ocean, but Nick and Kelsey had tuned him out, digging the trench between them deeper until it became a gulf.

Nick didn't know why he was so averse to making up with his best friend. It certainly wasn't the first time Kelsey had intervened in his life, and it wouldn't be the last. And, if he were being honest, the breakup with Tisha had been coming for a long time. Kelsey's action only sped up the timeline. And it wasn't as if he didn't agree with him; Ashleigh was all wrong for him. He shouldn't see her anymore. Why, then, was he so angry?

"I don't suppose there's any movement," Kelsey said.

Truck, who was taking his turn at the scope, shook his head.

"Why am I not surprised? I'm beginning to think this was a bogus mission. What's our intel?" he asked, directing the question to Nick because he had received the briefing. Nick had already briefed his team, but he couldn't blame Kelsey for double checking. They was also the first words he had directed at him since they left US soil three days ago.

"It's an optional target mission," Nick said. These were the hardest kind, the ones that put the most pressure on him as the team leader. He not only had to identify his target, he had to decide whether or not to make the kill. "There's a lot of activity swirling here, but the CIA hasn't been able to get precise info."

Kelsey made a "Pfft" sound. None of them held a lot of trust in the CIA. Rationally Nick knew the intelligence agency could only depend on the locals they had turned, locals who usually proved to be less than reliable. But when it was their lives on the line, it was difficult not to feel resentment when they received shoddy intel.

"We're going to have to do our own recon," Nick added. He had hoped they might learn what they needed to know by waiting and watching, but the encampment was closed up tight with only a few villagers coming and going. Nick thought perhaps they were delivering food or other supplies and were probably innocent bystanders. Some of them might be operatives the CIA were getting their information from. If so, then he could see why the info was so spotty. The place was a ghost town, as if the inhabitants sensed they were being watched and were taking every precaution.

"Finally," Kelsey said. "Good thing I brought my Arabian-woman disguise. All the fellas swoon when I don my burka. Mata Hari Kelsey, that's what they call me."

The rest of the team ignored him, as they usually did. Kelsey was Nick's spotter and as long as they had Lolly and Truck, he would stay behind with Nick. Plus, Lolly was the best at recon and Truck had the best ear for languages. While all of them had memorized a few phrases during the war, Truck could maintain and understand actual conversations, one of the major reasons he was placed as a machine gunner on such an elite team.

They had nothing but their weapons and the packs on their backs. Their one and only radio was hidden at the drop zone, and they would only use it to signal an airlift when they were ready to leave. It was too risky to carry radios whose signals could be intercepted or detected. Technology won and lost wars as well as saved or cost lives. Radios could either be a helpful lifeline or a dead giveaway. With few exceptions, the team almost never used radios while on assignment. When they needed communicate when they were separated, they used a series of hand signals or calls. There was no way to communicate with backup because there was no backup. It was the nature of the job that they were on their own. As such, they had learned to become resourceful. Lolly didn't have a way of getting close to the camp, but he would think of something, Nick was sure. He had done it a hundred times before, and he would do it a hundred times again. And he would find something for Ashton, or Ashton would find something for himself. Ashton was good at recon—they all were because they weren't part of a recon platoon for nothing—but Lolly had some sort of preternatural gift when it came to blending in.

Nick took over the scope as Truck and Lolly faded into the scenery. It was uncanny the way they were there one minute and gone the next. How did Lolly *do* that?

"So, uh, I noticed you didn't call the PK to say goodbye. I thought you would, after Tisha and all," Kelsey said.

"Are we really doing this now?" Nick asked.

"What else is there to do?"

"Anything but this," Nick said. He wasn't one to discuss his emotions on the best of days, but especially not when he couldn't understand them himself. He missed Ashleigh, really missed her, with an ache he had never felt before, and it scared him.

"Look, you know I was right," Kelsey said.

Nick's natural inclination was to spin and pin him with a stare, but that would involve leaving watch duty, so he settled for a surly tone. "Why do I know you're right?"

"Because you didn't call her. You haven't seen her. You're letting her go."

"Am I?" Nick asked.

"You should," Kelsey said, his voice getting angry.

"Why do you care so much?"

"Because I don't like to see you throw your life away on some woman."

"Throw it away?" Nick repeated. "How would I be throwing it away?" Nick knew the answer, but he couldn't stand to hear it from Kelsey's lips.

"She's not the woman for you; she's too high maintenance. She'll require everything. First it'll be your beer and poker nights, and the next thing you know she's demanding you give up the corps because the life is too hard or the job is too dangerous. It's always something with women like that."

Nick's hand tightened on the scope. He didn't like the way Kelsey said *with women like that* as if there was something wrong with Ashleigh. There was nothing wrong with Ashleigh. "I mostly gave up beer a long time ago already." He hadn't wanted to take any chances on messing up his career. Too much alcohol made him unpredictable and also made his hands shake. A sniper with shaky hands was no good to anyone. "I don't play poker much. And as for the corps, I don't think Ashleigh would ever ask that of me."

"But if she did, would you do it? Would you give it up?"

He thought that over. If he were with Ashleigh, really with her, as in a lifetime commitment, and the corps was too much for her, would he give it up? He didn't like the direction of his thoughts, and neither did Kelsey apparently.

"I can't even believe you're thinking about it," Kelsey exploded. "This woman has wormed her way into your brain like a virus. The answer is no, no you would not give up a career you've worked years for. Not for a woman, not for anything. If so, then what has this all been about?"

"I don't know," Nick answered honestly. "I mean, why did we take this job?"

"Because it's the best. Because it's the most elite of the most elite, and we wanted to prove to ourselves we could do it," Kelsey said.

"We did that. We're in. We made it; we're the best. Now what?" Nick asked. He wasn't being flippant; he was actually hoping Kelsey might have the answer.

"Now we work until we're either killed or miraculously make it to retirement," Kelsey said.

"Is that enough for you?" It had been enough for him once. Why wasn't it anymore?

"Yes," Kelsey said. "Because what else is there? Marriage? A family?" He paused to give a derisive snort. "How often does that work out? Someday down the road I'll probably get some woman knocked up and I'll be a part time dad to a really expensive kid. In fact, I should start garnishing my wages now for child support, but I'm not going to marry the woman. I'm not going to lose my head, my career, or my heart because it's not worth it."

"What about Melly?" Nick asked.

Kelsey sucked in a breath as if he'd been sucker punched. "What about Melly?"

"What if you marry Melly?"

"I'm not going to marry Melly," Kelsey insisted.

"You love her," Nick said.

"Of course I love her. She's my best friend, present idiot excluded. But I would never marry her."

"What if she marries someone else?"

"She's not going to marry someone else," Kelsey said, becoming irate all over again. Nick had never seen him in such a bad mood before. "We're twenty fricken seven years old, Lassiter. Pull yourself together and snap out of it. If you decide to have this mental breakdown in a decade, then maybe I'll be okay with it. But not now. Not when there's still too much fun to be had."

"Newsflash, buddy: I haven't had fun for a long, long time." When was the last time he hadn't felt the weight of the world pressing on his shoulders? When was the last time he had felt purpose, direction, and a sense of rightness with his world? Had he ever? He had spent a lot of years working and training to become a sniper, but he had reached his goal and now what? Was this all there was? Dedicate his life to the corps with nothing to show for it but a few notches on his confirmed-kills belt? Shouldn't there be something more? Shouldn't he be doing this for someone else besides himself? Shouldn't he be building a life for himself that didn't involve a rifle? An image of Ashleigh popped into his head, heavily pregnant with his child, and the sudden ache inside him burned like acid because he wanted it with a sickening amount of desperation. His hand shook on the scope, and he took a deep steadying breath.

Kelsey noticed, of course. "You are losing it, man." His tone was full of disgust. He gave his pallet an angry kick and lay down, falling into an instant sleep that left Nick alone with his torturous thoughts. It was a relief when his six hour watch was over and he could take his turn going to sleep. The beauty of being exhausted on a job was that insomnia was never a problem. He closed his eyes and the world faded instantly to black.

Six hours was the perfect amount of time. Four hours on the scope was ideal, eight hours was too long and the eye became fatigued. Six hours was stretching it, but it was also the right amount of sleep. They had perfected the formula over lots of missions with trial and error. But when Kelsey nudged Nick with his boot to take over his turn at the scope, six hours felt much, much too short. Still, he came instantly awake as he stood and reached for the scope.

It was uncanny how six hours of unconsciousness could feel like thirty seconds while six hours staring through a scope felt like a lifetime. Maybe it was because nothing moved—no wind, no sand, no animals, no humans. Nothing. Only years of discipline kept Nick's mind focused on what he was doing. It would be so easy to let his eye slack and his mind drift, but he didn't because Murphy's Law of soldiering declared the minute you lost focus, something vital happened. So he remained alert for the full six hours, handed the scope to Kelsey, and fell into an exhausted heap on the floor. Mental exhaustion was as daunting as physical exhaustion, if not more so. Civilians believed being a soldier meant being physically strong and capable, but they were wrong. So much of being a soldier was a mind game, something Nick had learned long ago. It was why little guys like Lolly were often the best soldiers— because nothing touched their minds. It was why soldiers were so compartmentalized—there was always a reserved part of the brain no enemy could reach. The problem came when they kept that portion closed off from everyone, including the people closest to them.

Nick shut off his deep thoughts before they could consume him and sank into a grateful sleep. It seemed like less than a minute later when Kelsey nudged him awake.

"That wasn't six hours," Nick said. He had an internal alarm clock, one all of them shared after being in so many time zones.

"It was four," Kelsey said. "We have movement."

Nick rolled to his feet in one fluid motion, taking the scope from Kelsey. The camp was suddenly bustling with activity. He blinked away the last of his sleep as he tried to process. What were they doing? It didn't appear as though they were prepping for a mission. The outing had a festive quality, like playtime in the prison yard. Were they simply stretching their legs and getting some air? But why all at once? What had drawn them out?

Then Nick saw it –a group of merchants, their wares set up like a market place. There was food and clothing, as if a caravan of salesmen had come calling at the camp.

"I think I found our target," Kelsey said. "The one with the table of fruit."

"A merchant?" Nick asked, though it would make sense. If the boss came in under the guise of being a merchant, then he could come and go under the radar. It would also explain why everyone was assembled outside.

"There's something about him. He's not what he appears to be. I think you should take the shot while you have it so we can get out of here. I'm starting to get a bad vibe about this mission."

Nick trusted Kelsey. Even his vibes that occasionally showed up and signaled trouble. But something held him back this time. Kelsey was right; there was something off about the merchant. But what if he was simply nervous? He had to know who he was dealing with. One wrong move and the people who were buying his wares would kill him. Still, he had an air about him, more confident than fearful, and he didn't hold himself like the others. The difference was there, but it was subtle. While Nick was thinking it over, Kelsey assembled his rifle and handed it over. Nick didn't prop it on the sill, however. He held it slack at his side while he continued to study the merchant.

"What are you waiting for?" Kelsey asked. "That's the target, and we both know it. Get this over with, and let's be done."

"Wait," Nick said.

"Wait for what?" Kelsey didn't usually argue. He was good about letting Nick lead. In fact, he usually seemed relieved Nick was the one making the tough calls. Nick knew this argument was about more than the target, though. This was a continuation of everything wrong between them lately. "I'm your spotter. Doesn't that mean anything? I spot the target, and you shoot it. Isn't that how it works? Don't you trust me to make decisions? Do we need to switch it up? Do you need me to take the shot because you've suddenly gone soft?"

Nick tried to tune him out, staring intently through the scope again. He handed the scope to a mutinous Kelsey. "Look at his face."

Kelsey took a cursory glimpse. "Yeah, I see it. So what? He's not going to have it much longer."

"Take a closer look," Nick instructed.

Kelsey pressed the scope closer to his eye, sighing expressively before letting loose a streak of curse words that would have curled a nun's hair. "I'm going to kill him," Kelsey said.

"You almost did," Nick pointed out. Lolly was their merchant. He had never been so brazen before as to walk into an encampment. If the insurgents noticed his dark skin and hair were more Mexican than Arabian, then he was a goner. He had covered his head and face with mud and a cloth, presumably to keep the dust away. But he hadn't covered up his natural confidence, which was what had tipped Kelsey off. If he didn't start looking a whole lot more subservient, he was going to be caught.

Kelsey cursed again. "Where do you think Truck is?"

"He's got to be close enough to hear what's going on. Underneath the fruit cart, maybe?"

Kelsey cursed again, and Nick felt like doing the same. They were sitting ducks down there. He lined up his rifle and looked through its scope, trying to get a feel for which one was the leader. Maybe he was absorbing Kelsey's paranoia, but he had a bad feeling things might begin to go downhill really quickly.

"C'mon, c'mon," he breathed. "Show yourself." Which one was calling the shots? They were all dressed the same, so he would have to go on mannerisms. Which one exuded confidence? Sometimes that could be deceiving, too, because there were those whose cockiness was unfounded. Over the years, though, Nick had become adept at picking out the subtle difference, distinguishing who was leading and who was following. Maybe because he was a leader he knew what to look for. Unbidden, Ashleigh's words sprang to his mind. Was he a natural leader? He hadn't thought of himself that way. He thought he adapted because it was what the job called for, but maybe his destiny had been written in the stars all along. Maybe he actually had what it took to be a leader of men, more than the three who were assigned to his team.

It was while his thoughts were on a tangent he found the man. He stood slightly apart, observing through narrowed eyes that missed nothing. He was calculating, cool, thoughtful. There were others who were loudly yelling orders and commands, but the quiet one was the leader, Nick knew it. "There," he said.

Kelsey followed the line of his vision with the scope. "Yep. You gonna take it?"

"Soon," Nick said. "What's my calculation?"

Kelsey put down the scope, licked his finger, and stuck it out the window. It was an old-school way of calculating wind velocity and direction, but they couldn't always rely on modern technology, especially not in the middle of nowhere. Kelsey did the math in his head. "Southwest, twenty miles per hour. Target is..." he squinted, reassuring himself of the distance. "Eight hundred." Eight hundred meters was far, but not impossible. The real problem would come after he took the shot. Nick began to debate with himself over whether or not he should wait until Truck and Lolly were out of harm's way first, but then the target made the decision for him. He turned his narrowed eyes on Lolly and began to point a finger in his direction as he opened his mouth. Before he could utter a word, his head dissolved into pink mist, blown to vapor by Nick's shot.

The scene erupted into mass chaos. Behind him, Kelsey began quickly packing their gear. Nick reloaded and covered Lolly and Truck as they made their escape. If anyone so much as turned questioningly in their direction, it would be the last thing they ever did.

There was too much pandemonium, however, for them to elicit suspicion. Once Nick was satisfied they were safe, he disassembled his weapon and packed it, helping Kelsey sweep the house to erase any trace of their presence. The last thing they wanted was to leave behind trash that would indicate marines had been in the area. There would be a lot of speculation over the assassination, but there would be no proof—Nick's team would make sure of it.

They finished and began the sprint to the drop zone, using the chaos as cover instead of waiting until night. Soon the encampment would begin to regroup, and then they would fan out in pursuit of their leader's killer. Nick planned to be in the air by then, or possibly in another time zone. But his body wasn't keeping pace with his mind.

Their arrival had been by parachute. They had done a dead drop and crept to their hideout. It had hurt Nick's still-tender backside, but that was nothing compared to running at top speed, loaded down with full gear. His wound burned. There was a good chance he was going to need new stitches after this, and the pain was intense. He couldn't afford to take it slowly, though. If he slowed down, then Kelsey would slow down to keep pace, and they might not make it. So he closed his mind to the pain and focused on pumping his legs, up, down, up, down. On and on he ran for miles through the rocky terrain until his lungs burned as much as the wound in his behind.

Kelsey reached the drop zone first and began clearing away the dirt and debris from the radio's hiding spot. He picked up the radio and gave the request for a pickup, along with their coordinates. The chopper was ten minutes out. There was nothing to do but sit and wait for Lolly and Truck to catch up with them.

Nick stood still and breathed deeply. He wasn't sure if the liquid trickling down his leg was sweat or blood. Exactly how much damage had he done to the sutures that were beginning to heal? Whatever happened, it wouldn't be fatal, and was therefore bearable. His breathing had started to return to normal again when there was a burst of gunfire from the opposite direction. From the sound, they knew it was Truck. Since there was no return fire, they knew it was a warning instead of an actual engagement. They were probably being pursued. Kelsey's gun was already out. Nick's rifle was packed, but it wouldn't do him much good anyway since it was a slow-action weapon. Instead he withdrew his sidearm.

The chopper came within hearing distance, and this was the part Nick hated the most. Because he was armed with only a handgun, he would have to be the first one on the plane. It was necessary, but it galled him to go first. Still, it was what it was and changing the plans so he could feel like a hero might get his team killed. So he stood still and ready, his weapon drawn, as he prepared to board the chopper as soon as it came within range.

The helicopter came into view at the same time Lolly and Truck did. They rounded a bend at an all-out sprint, which wasn't easy to do while holding automatic weapons, but they were doing it.

The chopper touched down and Nick boarded. Kelsey waited until Lolly and Truck were closer, and then two things happened at once. They caught sight of the mob chasing Lolly and Truck. It was difficult to tell how well they were armed in the melee of bodies, but it was a safe bet at least some of them were. Lolly kept sprinting while Truck paused to spray machine gun fire into the approaching mob, catching some of them so a few were picked off. Then he began sprinting again while Nick and Kelsey leaned out of the chopper, adding their own cover fire.

Lolly reached the aircraft and shoved his weapon into Nick's hands. "Go," he said. The pilot looked at Nick for confirmation, and Nick gave him a nod as Lolly hooked his legs around the edge of a bench and dangled upside down. They began to ascend and Lolly caught Truck's wrist with both hands, yanking him up as Kelsey laid down a blanket of cover fire.

Truck scrambled inside then he and Nick reached over to pull Lolly up. "Geez, kid, is there anything you can't do?" Nick asked. He had worked with the guy for three years and never seen him pull an acrobatic stunt like that before.

Lolly grinned, all blushing modesty, at least until Truck spoke.

"Yeah, there's one thing he can't do, and it involves a woman." But he slapped Lolly's back in a show of appreciation.

"So, for the record, is flexibility a family trait? I mean, can Melly do what you just did?" Kelsey asked.

Lolly lost his smile. He held up his left hand. "Here's you." He held up is right hand, far away. "Here's the line you crossed. Go back."

Kelsey held up his hands in mock surrender. "I'm curious about my friends' abilities. Can't blame a guy for asking."

Nick leaned back against the cool metal wall of the helicopter. Now that it was over, his adrenaline was beginning to crash. Usually the crash came much later, but he suspected his recent injury was partly to blame for his total lack of energy.

"Uh, Whit, your bum is blushing," Kelsey said.

"What?" Nick asked.

"You're bleeding," Lolly translated. "When we get back, I'm going to have to look at that." In addition to everything else, Lolly was the one with the most medical training. He had dreams of being a paramedic when he left the marines.

"You little multi-tasker," Kelsey said, giving him a pat on the head.

Anyone else would have snapped Kelsey's hand from his wrist for such a patronizing action, but Lolly merely shooed his hand away with an annoyed frown.

"It's fine," Nick assured him. "I tore the stitches a little."

"If you say so," Lolly muttered.

Nick closed his eyes again, allowing his thoughts to drift. Like always lately they drifted to Ashleigh, but this time he found he didn't mind so much. In fact, as he pictured her smile and remembered their one too-brief kiss, he found he didn't mind at all.

CHAPTER 17

Home. It wasn't much, but there was a bed with no scorpions and food with no gritty sand in every bite. There was total relaxation with no danger of discovery or death. After plane hopping for twenty six hours and a debriefing that lasted four—followed by a trip to the doctor with a whole bunch of head shaking and nine new stitches--Nick was exhausted. He slept for eighteen hours straight, and when he woke he was disoriented. He knew he was home, but he had no idea what day it was, let alone what time. His clock read eight, but he had blackout curtains, so it might have been eight at night or eight in the morning.

The bathroom was ablaze with light from the window, alerting him to the fact that it was morning. He stumbled into the shower and stood under the spray for a long time. When was the last time he showered? He honestly couldn't remember. It was the day before the mission began, but how many days ago was that? How many days since he saw Ashleigh? That was the real question his brain was trying to come up with. And—even more pressing—what was he going to do about it now that he was home?

He couldn't call her after more than a week's absence and pick up where they left off, wherever that was. She had to know they had been out of town because Lolly told them upon their return to the states she and Melly were becoming good friends. They had spent nearly every day together during the team's absence. Lolly was glad for the connection, and so was Nick because it meant Ashleigh knew they were out of the country. Maybe she would worry about him. Maybe he would be given a free pass for making no attempt to contact her before or since the mission.

He had just finished shaving when his phone rang. He picked it up and frowned when the caller ID showed it was Ashleigh. She didn't seem the stalking type. In fact, he had been looking forward to pursuing her, if that was what he decided to do. Seeing her name on his phone was so disappointing he almost didn't answer, but he supposed he owed her an explanation for his total disappearance.

"Hello."

"Hello, is this Nick?"

The voice didn't belong to Ashleigh, and Nick's frown deepened. "Yes."

"This is Caleigh, Ashleigh's sister. I...I'm not sure I'm doing the right thing here. Ashleigh would probably kill me for calling, but I thought you might want to know. She's in the hospital."

He gripped the phone tighter, his breath coming in short gasps. "What happened?"

"Someone put one of those homemade bombs in her truck this morning, you know what I mean? The kind you make in a soda bottle? Only they put some nails and stuff in it. It went off when she was sitting right beside it."

"Is...is she alive?" In his world, bomb plus shrapnel often equaled death.

Caleigh seemed surprised by the question. "Sure. She had a nail in her leg and some other cuts and scratches, but she's going to be fine. That's probably why she didn't call, but I'm worried about her and...I don't know. You seem capable of taking care of her. I think she needs you."

Nick's emotions were definitely on a roller coaster because his earlier fear quickly plummeted to guilt. He should have been there. He should have gone to her house this morning and talked. If he had, he would have noticed the MacGyver bomb. She could have died because he had been too frightened to face her, to face whatever was between them.

"I'll be there in a few minutes," he said, his voice raw with emotion and fear.

"She's going to kill me," Caleigh added. "She's not exactly the type to call a guy, especially when she has an actual need. But… She's been different since she met you. Better than after Charlie. It was nice to see her like this again. And then this week, she was so…I think you're good for her. There, I've officially said too much, but that's sort of my lot in life. Don't tell Ashleigh." With that, she ended the call.

Nick stared at his silent phone, dazed. How had his world become so upside down he was shot at Starbucks and someone placed an explosive device in Ashleigh's car? These things weren't supposed to happen here in the real world. He trained to be ready for any situation, but he expected those situations to happen somewhere far away, and not in his own town, not to Ashleigh.

Snapping himself out of his mental fog, he drove to the hospital, cursing himself for not finding out where she was. The emergency room was a safe bet unless she had needed surgery to remove the shrapnel from her leg. He started with the ER and saw Reverend Desmond sitting in the waiting area.

"Mr. Desmond, sir, how is she?" Nick said.

The pastor looked up, startled at seeing Nick. "Ashleigh called you?"

"Caleigh did," Nick replied.

"Oh." His expression told Nick this wasn't happy news, but Nick knew it couldn't be easy to think of Ashleigh lying injured on a gurney somewhere. If it wasn't easy for him, then how much must her father be faring?

"Would it be okay if I see her?" He was anxious to assure himself Ashleigh was okay. Perhaps he was more battle weary than he realized because the anxiety in his chest wouldn't be quelled until he saw Ashleigh conscious and in one piece.

"I don't think that's a good idea," Reverend Desmond replied as his wife emerged from the emergency room.

"Nick, what are you doing here? How nice of you to come. Why don't you go on back and say hello to Ashleigh? I'm sure she would like to see you."

Nick stood looking between husband and wife before deciding his desire to see Ashleigh outweighed his desire to make a good impression on Reverend Desmond. He turned his back on the man, following Mrs. Desmond through the swinging doors to Ashleigh. He braced himself to see her and even though she didn't look that bad, the sight of her lying on a hospital bed gripped his stomach with icy fear.

There was a large bandage on her leg, three smaller ones on her arms, and a few light burns from the chemicals. Her forehead had a small gash, and so did one of her cheeks. Nick knew she was lucky; a bomb was unpredictable, especially one that had been enhanced with debris. She might have lost an eye or had severe chemical burns. Even though she seemed relatively unharmed, he still wanted to sweep her into his arms and carry her somewhere safe, somewhere hidden where he would be sure to protect her.

When the curtain opened, she turned weary eyes to her mother who bustled in and began fussing over her, arranging her thin blanket and pushing her hair off her face. Her eyes quickly skimmed past her mother and landed on Nick. If he hadn't been so alarmed at the sight of her in a hospital bed, he would have smiled at her expression. Her eyes narrowed enough to let him know she was angry with him and trying to hide it. His absence had hurt her, but she would die before she let him see. Maybe it was the anger or the pride and stubbornness, Nick didn't know. All he knew was at that moment everything in his world came to a crashing halt and reoriented itself on the woman now staring him down. Oh, yeah, this was going to be fun.

"Nick," Ashleigh said, tipping her head coolly in his direction. Nick wouldn't have thought it was possible for anyone to look regal and dismissive while her mother was fussing over her bandages like a worried hen, but somehow Ashleigh pulled it off.

"Nick came to see you, honey," Mrs. Desmond said. She sounded as nervous and anxious as she looked as she continued to bustle about the small space, easing from side to side in a vain attempt to make sure the sheet was even on each side of Ashleigh. Caleigh stood in the small space, too, looking as anxious as her mother as she shifted from foot to foot and wrung her hands. These two women were cut from the same high-strung cloth. Ashleigh was like her father—steady and strong. She apparently felt it her duty to keep her mother and sister calm.

"Mom, I'm fine. Really. It doesn't even hurt. You can stop doing that. Mom, put the blanket down. I'm covered. Caleigh, sit down and stop squirming. Really, guys, I'm fine. It's a few scratches."

At last Nick couldn't stand it anymore. "Could I have a few minutes alone with Ashleigh, please?"

Mrs. Desmond froze and looked at him, considering. "Okay," she said at last. "But you call if you need anything, Ash. We're right outside. I can get you some more medicine, or water, or food. Are you hungry? You must be hungry."

"I'm not hungry, Mom. I'm fine."

"Come on, Mom," Caleigh said. She grasped her mother's arm and began tugging her away, looking more than a little relieved at the sight of Nick.

He waited until they were outside the curtain, and then he stepped forward and took Ashleigh's face in his hands. Her eyes were full of astonishment, her mouth opened as if ready to protest, so he kissed her before she could utter a word. He wondered what her reaction would be, but it was better than he could have hoped because she reached for him, plunging her fingers into his hair as she pulled him close and returned the kiss with unbridled fervor. Blood began rushing and roiling through him, as if he was back on assignment and all synapses were firing on full alert. It had never been like this with a woman, had never come close to anything like this. To think he had found this sort of unbridled and explosive chemistry with someone so good and kind and lovely was beyond his wildest dreams. This was better than any adrenaline rush; this was better than anything. At least until Ashleigh came to her senses and pushed him away.

"What are you doing?" she exclaimed, panting slightly as she tried to catch the breath he'd stolen. She pressed the back of her wrist to her tender lips and blinked to clear her gauzy expression. "You can't go away without a word, come back, and do that."

"Why not? That's what marines do after an assignment. Welcome to the corps." He leaned against the post to his right. He was probably coming off cocky, but it was hard not to feel cocky after a kiss like that.

"You have a girlfriend," she whispered. Her eyes were downcast now, and the light bulb went off. Ashleigh felt *guilty.* Even though she had barely met Tisha and they had only shared that one innocent kiss, she had been eating her heart out with grief over her naughty behavior. He couldn't help it—he laughed.

"Man, you are such a good person," he said, shaking his head. "What are you doing with a guy like me?"

"I'm not with you," Ashleigh said, stubbornly holding on to her anger. She crossed her arms over her chest and gave him what would have been a frosty expression if it hadn't been laced with blatant longing that eventually settled on his lips and lingered.

"Newsflash, sweetheart: you are." He eased closer and kissed her again, because he knew he could. His hands settled on her waist as hers slipped around his neck—at least until she came to her senses and shoved him away again.

"Stop doing that."

"Why? Don't you like it?"

She opened her mouth to answer, thought better of it, and tried again. "It's not right."

"Why not?" Nick asked, the picture of total innocence.

"You have a girlfriend."

"No, I don't."

"Oh." The guilty frown was back. "I'm sorry." She sounded so miserable he almost laughed again, but this time he wisely refrained.

"It's really not your fault. The relationship was doomed from the start and our breakup was inevitable. Better now than before I became any more vested."

"Oh." She sat back, struggling to think of another excuse. "Still, it's wrong."

"Why?" Nick asked.

She shrugged one shoulder and winced when she was reminded of her many cuts and scrapes. "It just is. We don't fit."

"Why not?" Nick asked. "Don't you like me, Ash?" He gave her the puppy dog eyes—brown eyes were definitely good for some things.

"Of course I do," she said, tearing her gaze away from his penetrating one.

"And we're crazy attracted to each other. I mean, the chemistry is of the charts."

"Yeah, but…that's not…that's not what having a relationship is all about," Ashleigh protested.

"If it's not about liking each other and being attracted to each other, then what is it about?" Nick said. "I'm confused." He perched on the edge of her bed and reached for her hand, toying with her fingers. "Explain it to me." He threw in the puppy dog look again for good measure, and Ashleigh groaned.

With effort, she ripped her fingers from his clutch and sat on them. "Stop this. You were gone, and I made peace with that. I found closure. You can't come in here and upset that closure."

He placed his palms on either side of her and leaned in. "You want me to go away?"

"What is that thing you're doing with your eyes?" she whispered.

"What thing?" he asked, as if he hadn't spent forever perfecting the technique.

"The thing where you look like Oliver Twist and I'm the mean matron withholding your bowl of gruel."

"You're too book smart; most of that reference was over my head." He pushed his luck, leaning in a little more until only a centimeter separated his lips from hers. This time she would kiss him, he had to nudge her a little further.

He miscalculated Ashleigh's stubbornness, however. She leaned away, pressing herself into the mattress. "Don't do this to me, Nick," she pled.

"What?" he asked.

"Toy with me."

He leaned back, some of his enthusiasm dimming. "What? Who says I'm toying with you."

"I do," she said, gaining confidence as he lost it.

"Why would I be toying with you?"

"Because you're you, and I'm me."

"What's that supposed to mean?" he asked. He was becoming angry now.

"It means you could have any woman on the planet, and probably have. And I'm me. I'm the freckle-faced girl who should probably marry a missionary."

"Is that who you want? A missionary?" he asked. "Because I was under the impression you were over being dogmatic and judgmental. Or was that all talk? When push comes to shove, do you not want to be with someone like me?"

"How could you…" she began, but the curtain was shoved aside as her mother returned. Her mother fussed and clucked around them while Nick and Ashleigh stared at each other in sullen silence. Ashleigh was doing some eye tricks of her own. Anger made her usually muddy-green color pop with amber highlights he found fascinating. She was beautiful. Had he found her merely cute a few weeks ago? Amazing.

"You'll feel all better when I get you home and into bed," Mrs. Desmond was saying.

"What?" Ashleigh said. Reluctantly, she tore her gaze off Nick to focus on her mother.

"I said we're going home. The doctor released you."

"No, Mom, I'm not going home. I'm going to work," Ashleigh said.

Her mother stared at her, mouth agape, as if she had announced she was going to go punch kittens for laughs. "No way, Ashleigh. You're going home where I can take care of you."

Nick could hear Ashleigh's inward groan, and he couldn't blame her. Mrs. Desmond's version of care was stifling. "Mom, I'm so close to my deadline at Henry's house. I don't want to disappoint him."

Henry? When had the odious Mr. Baker become Henry? Nick's jealousy flared to immediate heights. "It's okay, Mrs. Desmond," Nick replied. "I'll go with her and keep an eye on her."

Now it was Ashleigh's turn to bristle. "Keep an eye on me?"

"Yes," Nick said. "To keep an eye on you. You're banged up. I'll make sure you don't work too hard." *And I'll make sure no one else tries to blow you up.*

"You're not coming to work with me," Ashleigh said. She set her face in the drill sergeant expression, and Nick quelled for the first time. He hadn't yet won a round with her when she looked like that. But he couldn't lose this one; it was too important. If he let her push him away, he might never get close again. Fortunately, Mrs. Desmond was inadvertently on his side.

"It's either him or me, Ashleigh," she said. She crossed her arms over her chest and tipped her chin in the air, and Nick realized Ashleigh got her stubbornness from both her father and her mother. That must explain why it was so potent.

Ashleigh sagged in defeat. "Nick," she muttered. "I choose Nick."

Even though her tone was disgruntled, Nick smiled because he planned to hear those words on her lips again—the sooner, the better.

He stood back while her mother took over the process of getting her released. He had driven her car which had still been parked in his driveway for some reason, maybe because she had too much pride to come and retrieve it. Whatever the reason, he was glad he didn't have to hike himself into his truck in front of her. Maybe she wouldn't be able to gage the amount of pain he was in.

"You shouldn't be doing this," he said. "You should take the day off."

"Says the man who went who-knows-where after he was shot," Ashleigh said.

"That was different," Nick said.

"How so? Because your job is more important than mine? Maybe it is, but I still like to keep my word. I set a deadline for this job, and I intend to meet it."

She was spoiling for a fight, but he wasn't inclined to give her one, mostly because he felt almost euphorically happy to be with her again. "That wasn't it. I was going to say it's different because if I hadn't gone, then my sergeant would have made the rest of the team pay for it."

"That's not fair," Ashleigh said.

Nick had a good chuckle over that one. "Welcome to the marines."

"That's the second time you said that to me today, but it's not necessary. I have no plans to join anytime soon."

That's what you think, Nick thought, but he refrained from saying anything else that might set her off. "Did you tell the police your suspicions about your ex?"

"No."

His head swiveled to look at her. "Why not?"

"It didn't seem relevant."

"Didn't seem relevant? Someone tried to blow you up this morning and you don't think it's relevant to tell them you saw your abusive ex hanging around watching you a few weeks ago?"

"First of all, it's really not your business." He opened his mouth to debate that point, but she hurried on before he could. "Second, you saw how the police treated me when I shot you. I didn't think they would be inclined to believe me. Third, it doesn't matter anyway."

She sounded resigned, and his anger kicked up a notch. If he could get his hands on her ex... "What do you mean it doesn't matter? Of course it matters."

"No, it really doesn't. We both know if Charlie wanted me dead, then I would be dead by now."

He didn't disagree with her there, and that was what was sitting wrong for him. He couldn't figure out why a marine who knew how to kill people fifty different ways would choose an amateurish MacGyver bomb, but he also couldn't get a straight answer on the man's whereabouts. "I still don't get why you think it wouldn't matter," he said.

"Because it was a warning, a warning he's watching me, and a warning he can get close to me. If I hadn't seen the bomb a second before it went off, if the gearshift hadn't taken the brunt of the damage, if I hadn't turned toward the door and covered my face, who knows how much worse it could have been? Maybe he meant to disfigure me. But whether or not I told the police wouldn't matter because nothing makes any difference. I told the marines about the abuse, and they gave him a promotion. Why should I tell anyone else?"

Nick banged his fist on the steering wheel at the futility and frustration of it all. As long as he was around, he could attach himself to her for her own safety. But he wasn't often around. The higher ups were already hinting at the next mission in his future. There was always someone in the world who needed killed or spied on.

"The least I can do is make some phone calls, find out the whereabouts of your ex," Nick said.

"Nick, I appreciate the offer, but you don't have to. I don't want you getting involved in this."

"Baby, I couldn't be any more involved," he said and then watched as she tried to figure out the cryptic comment, her hands twisting nervously in her lap as she studiously avoided eye contact. She was so different from the women he was used to. More often than not he felt like the proverbial raccoon being chased by a pack of crazed hounds. The women of his association made no secret of their intentions and weren't shy about making all the moves. Ashleigh was definitely making him work for it, and he found he liked being the pursuer for once. He was charmed by her mix of steel and reserve. She might go full throttle when she knew she was in the right, but when it came to men, she was a little uncertain. Her vulnerability sparked his protective instincts. How could he have considered letting her go, even for a moment? How had he let a small dose of fear keep him away from the best thing that had ever happened to him? There was no small amount of relief at having finally made up his mind. Now all he had to do was convince Ashleigh, and he looked forward to that prospect very much, which was why he pulled into Henry Baker's driveway and sat staring at her like an idiot, smiling.

"You're scaring me a little," Ashleigh admitted.

"Am I?" he asked totally unconcerned. "Why?"

"You're…intense. More intense than before you went away. Did something happen while you were gone?"

"Let me put it this way: You and I have something in common because once I make up my mind, there's no changing it." He wanted to kiss her again, but he had to remember this was Ashleigh. His relationship with her would be a marathon and not a sprint. It was time to put on the brakes and pull back, way back, like all the way to grammar school. So he tentatively reached over the console and took her hand. She let him, and his heart did a flip, the first time such an innocent action had ever brought him so much satisfaction. He had always lived on fast forward, always pushed his limits. For a lot of years, he and Kelsey had maintained a competition to see who could get a woman's clothes off the fastest. And now he was elated to be sitting in a car and holding hands. No wonder Kelsey was freaked out. Nick wasn't freaked out anymore, though. He was…what was he? What was this unknown feeling creeping through his veins? Contentment. Nick was content, and the encroaching peace felt better than he ever imagined.

Like all good things, the moment had to come to an end. This one did when Henry Baker abruptly ripped open the passenger door and stuck his head inside. "Ashleigh, are you okay? I was so worried when I got your call."

Nick's hand tightened on Ashleigh's hand. The doctor-to-be was feeling pretty chummy with Ashleigh. Nick didn't like that—he didn't like that at all. And if the way the man's gaze lingered on their joined hands was any indication, he didn't like Nick's presence, either.

"I'm fine, Henry, really," Ashleigh said. She tugged her hand from Nick's. *Henry* moved aside as she exited the vehicle, hovering the same way Mrs. Desmond had earlier. Nick's only satisfaction came from the fact that he knew Ashleigh didn't enjoy that sort of stifling attention.

"You didn't have to come today," Baker continued. "I would have understood the need to take a couple of days off and recuperate."

"I wanted to come," Ashleigh said. "I'm not good with down time, and I'm too goal oriented to leave a project unfinished."

Nick walked behind them—apparently forgotten—as they made their way to the house. He didn't mind because it was a good way to observe. What he saw eased his jealousy. Henry Baker might be eating his heart out for Ashleigh, but the feeling wasn't mutual.

"Yes, you're a hard worker," Henry said, bestowing a goofy grin on Ashleigh. At least Nick thought it looked goofy. He was going about it all wrong by basically throwing himself at her, but since it didn't appear to be working it was really none of Nick's concern. Unless—how far was the egghead willing to go in his pursuit of Ashleigh? Was he stalking her? Had he placed the bomb in some sort of misguided attempt to gain her attention? The question bore looking into, but Nick had his doubts the Nutty Professor could actually assemble and plant a bomb without blowing himself up. The act required not only cunning, but a certain amount of athleticism because MacGyver bombs had no timer. Whoever had assembled it had to have done so somewhere nearby, timed it right before Ashleigh left the house, and then run away and hidden before it could go off. The doctor seemed like more of a calculating planner, not given to fast action.

"Whoa, Ash, this looks great," Nick said, stopping short in front of her creation. It amazed him she had made the built-in out of a few pieces of lumber. In the beginning, when she had described what she was going to do, he hadn't been able to picture it. Now he was seeing her work in person, and even without any training he could recognize the quality in her craftsmanship.

"Thank you," Ashleigh said. She turned a beaming smile on him, the first one she had bestowed since their reunion and they got caught up staring at each other a few beats before the annoying Henry cleared his throat a few times.

"You need a tissue?" Nick asked.

Ashleigh's smile changed to a warning frown, as if to remind him the geek was her employer, at least for the foreseeable future. He pressed his lips together and turned in a slow circle, surveying the interior of the house for clues about Mr. Baker's state of mind. The more he took in, the less convinced he became the man had anything to do with Ashleigh's attack. It was possible the man was crazy, what with his large collection of bone fragments, but if he were going to break the law, he would go full throttle like one of those serial killers people wrote books about. He would want to make a name for himself by displaying his intelligence. He wouldn't place a homemade bomb in someone's truck and wait for it to go "BOOM!" Still, it was worth making his presence known as Ashleigh's protector. For that reason he stood in the background, silent and menacing as Ashleigh worked and Henry watched with an adoring smile on his pale face.

If Ashleigh felt frustrated or intimidated with two men standing around watching her work, she didn't show it. Nick tried to give her a reprieve by calling his contacts in the corps to try and determine the whereabouts of Charlie-the-ex. Despite having served for nine years, his contact list was pitiful, a situation he intended to remedy soon. That was something else he needed to discuss with Ashleigh, but they couldn't exactly have a conversation with Henry hovering nearby. Didn't the man have something to read or study? Nick was under the impression earning a doctorate was a full-time occupation, but Henry stood fawning over Ashleigh like he hadn't anything else to do. Not that Nick could blame him. There was something magnetic about watching her wield tools. Maybe it was the effortless yet total concentration she afforded every detail of her design. Or maybe it was the muscles in her sinewy arms. Whatever it was, Nick was having a hard time not staring as awestruck as Henry.

The day passed slowly for Ashleigh. She would never admit it, but the combined presence of Nick and Henry was almost too much. Henry with his perfectionistic precision that seemed to be judging her every move, and Nick with his hooded stares that could make her hands shake for a different reason. Henry tried to engage her in conversation that pulled her focus from her task while Nick spent much of the day on the phone trying to track down Charlie. All in all, it was a relief to call it a day, not to mention the fact that she was more sore and shaken than she had let on. Why did her body ache so? It wasn't as if she had been jarred in any way. Did panic always cause muscle aches? Because she had definitely panicked when she realized there was a bomb on the floorboard of her car. Her many cuts and bruises stung, too, reminding her of her close call.

Nick was quiet as he drove her back to her house. Propriety demanded she invite him inside, but she had no energy for proper manners. Not that she wasn't enjoying her time with him, because she was. Even silence was enjoyable with him. But Nick didn't want silence—he wanted to talk. About them. That was definitely something she wasn't up for. Right now she wanted a hot shower and her bed, not necessarily in that order.

But when he walked her to the door, he lingered as if he intended to say goodbye and leave. Irrational as it was since it was what she wanted, she was disappointed. And then he kissed her, and her disappointment fled along with all other rational thought. It was a simple kiss, very sweet, and very potent. As usual when she was with him, Ashleigh lost her head and leaned in, intending to kiss him again, but Nick pulled away.

"How about we continue this tomorrow?" he asked. "A real date, something not involving guns, bombs, or power tools."

Ashleigh wanted to say yes, but fear and common sense held her back. "I don't think that's a good idea, Nick." Why extend the torture? Why spend more time together when they both knew it was going to end badly? Plus there was the promise she had made herself that she would never, ever, ever date another marine.

Nick smiled and kissed her again, the cad. He knew she was totally defenseless. "I'll pick you up about this time tomorrow. Night, Ash."

Dazedly she stared after him as he walked away, belatedly coming to her senses. "That wasn't a yes," she called. He waved over his shoulder, but didn't turn around. Ashleigh forced herself to go inside the house, a better alternative than watching him drive away like the heartsick idiot she was.

CHAPTER 18

The next day was not a good one for Ashleigh. Her body was sore, her mind distracted, and her spirit out of sorts. For the first time, Henry's hovering annoyed her, and she had to hold herself in check to keep from snapping at him. She supposed she should be grateful for his solicitous attitude; it was the only reason her parents had let her out of the house that morning.

"He hovers over me all day," she told her father. "No one could possibly get to me with him there. If you don't believe me, ask Nick." To her chagrin, he had. She sat mortified over her bowl of cereal while her father called Nick and asked his opinion on the matter. That was when she knew for certain it was time to get her own place. Her parents had good intentions, but she was a grown woman. Their overprotective behavior bordered on the ridiculous.

By the time she arrived home, her bad mood had only increased. Her car was in the driveway, which meant Nick was there. Ashleigh bolted from her truck that still smelled like drain cleaner and stomped inside. There were voices in the kitchen, so she headed that way but stopped short in the doorway at the sight of Nick sitting at the table, sipping sweet tea while he talked to her parents. The scene was both familiar and aggravating. Ashleigh's parents had always vetted her dates this way, by sitting them down at the kitchen table and putting them through a sort of interview. In high school, her rare dates had become even rarer once word spread of the mild interrogation. Charlie hadn't minded, though. He had charmed her parents; he had charmed them all. Now there was another handsome marine sitting in the same place and, if the looks on her parents' faces were any indication, he was winning them over, like Charlie.

"Hi, honey," her mother said. Her bright tone did little to hide the relief and worry in her face. Her father remained silent, his eyes scanning her for any trace of harm. Ashleigh gripped her hands into tight fists as Nick added his own inspection, though his look was much different than that of her father. He was amused by her bad mood if his unabashed smile was any indication. When she glanced at him, he added a wink to make sure she was good and riled up.

"Nick, what are you doing here?" She was proud of the way her tone remained cool and unaffected, even though what she really wanted to do was stamp her foot and tell them all to stop ogling her, stop stifling her, stop pursuing her, if that's what he was doing. She still wasn't sure what he was up to and after his lengthy disappearance, she wasn't sure she trusted him. Maybe she had never trusted him. Charlie was gone, but he had left his ghost behind, and it haunted her whenever she thought of being with another man, even Nick.

"I'm here for our date," Nick said. His eyes raked over her again. "Are you ready to go, or would you prefer to change?" He was wearing jeans and a nice shirt, one that pulled taught over his muscles and brought out the warm chocolate tones in his expressive eyes. In comparison, she looked exactly like someone who had been doing manual labor all day—sweaty and bedraggled, her hair half out of its ponytail, her tank top stained with glue and peppered with sawdust.

"I don't think I'm up for a date tonight," Ashleigh said, trying to word it carefully in front of her parents. The urge to have a full-scale temper tantrum was growing stronger.

"That's okay," Nick said, his unperturbed tone a sharp contrast to hers. "We can stay in. Gives us plenty of time to talk that way."

She took the words as the challenging ultimatum they were—they could either stay in and talk, or go out and not talk. It was her choice. She sighed in defeat, but if he thought she was done being angry with him, he was sadly mistaken. "Let me grab a quick shower," she said through tightly gritted teeth.

"Take your time," Nick said sweetly. "Your mom promised me some pie if I had to wait for you."

It's possible Ashleigh may have growled as she stalked toward the bathroom. He was being annoyingly sweet and patient when what she really wanted was a good fight. If he thought he could out-stubborn her, he was wrong. She refused to let down her guard again, to lose her head again, to lose her heart again. She had risked everything with Charlie, and she had lost. There was nothing left to wager on Nick who was a bad risk anyway because they were so mismatched. Why couldn't he see that? Why couldn't he see how wrong they were for each other? Being together would only lead to heartbreak, and Ashleigh already had enough heartbreak for a lifetime. She held on to the fact that he had left for his mission without a word. That had hurt. Surely that was proof of his character, wasn't it? He would only hurt her again if she let him, and she had no mind to let him.

Still, she dressed carefully for their date. He had only ever seen her in work clothes or casual attire. She could look good when she wanted to, and right now she wanted to very much. Maybe it was pride that fueled her desire to knock his socks off. If she thought about it, she would realize it was wrong to try and impress someone she intended to break up with, but she didn't let herself think too long on those lines. She simply wanted to look good, to redeem herself from too many ponytails, tank tops, and no makeup.

Caleigh was the beauty of the family, but Ashleigh wasn't without her merits, especially when she tried. She pulled out her little black dress, curled her hair so it hung in soft waves, and applied makeup more than her usual gloss and mascara. Despite her love of power tools and trucks, she liked to think of herself as a girly girl, but maybe she wasn't because after a cursory inspection of herself in the mirror, she turned away. A girly girl probably would have fussed more, but

Ashleigh had never been fussy. Like her father, she was usually ready in under a half hour and they waited together for her mom and Caleigh who always tried to outdo each other in the length of time it took to primp.

Nick was finishing his last bite of coconut pie when she entered the kitchen. He sputtered and choked, which was such a satisfying reaction she smiled, temporarily forgetting her determination to keep him at arm's length.

"Ready?" she asked. He nodded and took a sip of tea to try and regain normal breathing while Ashleigh stood back and enjoyed his discomfiture. Then he stood and the tables were turned because he was once again suave and in control as he said goodbye to her parents. He was such a gentleman as he complimented her mother on her pie and shook her father's hand it was as if he had been raised in the south all his life.

"How did you learn so much about southern manners?" she asked as he held the door to the house and waited for her to walk through.

"I spent a semester with a distant uncle in Georgia during my formative years. Those months were an invaluable lesson. I took my newly acquired manners to Minnesota with me the following year and had to beat the women away with my hockey stick. That was a golden time." He smiled as he held her car door, but Ashleigh frowned. The anecdote was a reminder that Nick had more experience than most men receive in a lifetime. He had dated more people than she had ever even known. Now he had turned his attention on her for whatever reason. This wasn't going to end well, and instinct told Ashleigh it would be she who would be left with a broken heart. She was in over her head because Nick was out of her league entirely.

He started the car, and she braced herself for *the talk*. She knew it was coming; it was only a matter of time. Her hands were clamped in her lap, waiting.

"Ashleigh," Nick said.

Here it comes. "Yes?"

"What's your favorite band?"

She sank into the seat, slightly deflated from the surprise. "I have a lot of them." Her statement came out sounding like a question. She tipped her head to study him. Was this some kind of trick? An elaborate lead in to *the talk?* "What's your favorite band?" The suspense was killing her. The sooner they got it over with, the better. Besides, she was still feeling in control. Now was the time to tell him it would never work. They could spend the evening together as friends, and that would be that.

"The Beatles. Doesn't everyone have to love the Beatles?" He paused, frowning. "Were you allowed to listen to the Beatles?"

"It so happens my dad loves the Beatles. Something you guys have in common. Who knew?"

"Your dad is an okay guy after you get past the terrifying part. I think we're going to get along well."

Ashleigh had her doubts about that, but she didn't voice them.

"What's your favorite movie?" Nick asked.

"I have a lot of those, too. I'm not the type of person who can pin down one favorite. For every question, I have an entire list."

"We've got all night. Let's hear it. Go back to the bands, though, because you never really answered, and I'm curious about your musical tastes."

Somehow they never got around to having *the talk* even though they never stopped talking. The discussion on music and movies led to books, board games, and sports. From there they diverged to cars, travel, and a discussion on which was better: winter or summer Olympics. It was exactly what a first date should be—light, fun, and so fast neither could believe when it was over.

That was Ashleigh's thought as Nick pulled into her driveway and walked her to the door. The night had seemingly been on warp drive. *Here it comes,* she warned herself again. He had lulled her into a false sense of security by avoiding the topic of them all night, but the night was over, and they were bound to have their long-awaited discussion.

Only they didn't. Nick used his finger to tip her face up to his and then he kissed her, so softly and sweetly Ashleigh was the one whose lips clung as he pulled away. He didn't embrace her, didn't touch her more than with his lips and one finger beneath her chin, but she felt as if he had caressed her. She shivered, waiting for she knew not what at this point.

"Same time tomorrow," Nick said. This time when he walked away she didn't protest. She didn't do anything at all except stare after him in numb stupefaction until her father turned on the light and poked his head out the door—a sure sign he had been waiting up for them.

CHAPTER 19

The next three nights were a repeat of the first. Nick was always waiting on her when she arrived home from Henry's house, talking in the kitchen with her mother like new best friends, always dressed in the same variation of jeans and a nice shirt. He waited while Ashleigh showered and got ready and then they went out.

He didn't take her anywhere out of the ordinary. The first night they went to a moderately priced restaurant and to a movie. The next night they had BBQ and played mini golf. On the third night he took her dancing, and that was special for Ashleigh.

"I haven't been dancing since my senior prom," Ashleigh commented.

"Your ex didn't take you dancing?" he asked.

She smiled because he sounded like dancing was part of every relationship when she knew few couples who went dancing for the fun of it. "No, Charlie wasn't much of a dancer."

"That should have been your first clue. Never trust a guy who can't dance," Nick said.

"My dad can't dance," Ashleigh said.

"Unless they're in the ministry. You didn't let me finish," Nick said.

He pulled her in close and his smile faded. "I'm not Charlie, Ash. I've never hit a woman, not even when they hit me. I'm bigger and stronger and it's never okay. I've never verbally abused anyone, and I've had some steaming fights in my lifetime."

She pressed his face between her palms so she could look deep into his fathomless brown eyes. "I know you're not him, Nick, I really do. I'm not afraid you're going to hit me or play with my mind."

"Then what? What are you so afraid of?"

It was the first time they had spoken of the issues between them all week. Nick had purposely kept things light and carefree, giving them time to get to know each other without the weight of the world bearing down. "In the same way getting slapped across the face leaves a hand mark, getting your heart broken leaves an imprint, too. I wish I could say I was brave and whole and read to take a chance, but I don't think I am."

"I'm not asking anything of you right now, Ashleigh. We're dancing. You can give me one dance, can't you?" Nick asked, his tone turning lighthearted again.

"Yes," Ashleigh said, which was an easy thing to say because Nick hadn't been exaggerating—he was a very good dancer.

After dancing, he took her to the ocean where they walked hand in hand along the beach. "Your mom wants to have a party tomorrow," Nick said.

"My mom would have a party every night if my dad would let her," Ashleigh said. "Did she invite you?"

"She invited everybody—me, Kelsey, Lolly, Truck, and Melly."

"Oh," Ashleigh said.

"You don't sound happy about it," Nick observed.

"No, it's…that's great," Ashleigh said. "I'm glad y'all will get a home-cooked meal for once."

"C'mon, Ash, what's bugging you?" Nick asked, giving her hand a little shake.

"Nothing. I love Melly; she's become a good friend in a short amount of time. And Lolly, too. He's adorable. If I had a little brother, I would want him to be like that—don't tell him I said that, though."

Lolly was a year older; he might not take kindly to being thought of as her younger sibling.

"It's Kelsey and Truck, isn't it?" Nick asked.

"I like them," Ashleigh rushed to assure him. "I'm not sure the feeling is mutual."

Nick's lack of reassurance was all the confirmation she needed. "It's not you," Nick said.

"Have they liked all your other..." she was going to say "girlfriends" and quickly amended it. "Women friends."

He looked down at her with a smile, probably guessing exactly how she had edited herself. "Yes."

"I thought so," she said, her tone dismal.

"Don't you see that's what makes you special?" Nick asked. "The other women were an interchangeable mass. Switch up their names, their features, it didn't matter because they were exchangeable, like paper dolls. But you are not like anyone who has come before. Kelsey knows, and he's afraid."

"And Truck," she pressed.

"Truck has his own issues. Something from his past he won't talk about. He neither likes nor trusts women. Believe me--with Truck it's not personal. He's like this with almost everyone who has two X chromosomes. Besides, they'll like you eventually. They have to."

"Why?" she asked.

"Because you're my girl." He dropped her hand and settled his arm around her shoulders. They walked on, talking and laughing, never suspecting someone was nearby watching and waiting.

* * *

Henry was hovering again. It was Friday, the last day of the job, and Ashleigh was already on edge. Tonight her mother was having the dinner for Nick's friends—ostensibly to get to know them, though her mother never needed a reason to entertain.

"Beautiful," Henry murmured for the hundredth time that day.

"Just beautiful." The way he was staring at her made her think maybe he wasn't talking about the cabinet.

Ashleigh finished loading up her tools and came back for the second half of her payment. Henry reluctantly handed her the envelope of cash. With the end of the job came the end of their relationship, such as it was. "Thank you, Henry."

"If I have any problems with the cabinet, can I call you?"

"What type of problems do you foresee?" Ashleigh asked, trying not to be peeved. She was a perfectionist, especially when it came to her work. She had checked and double checked the built-ins. They were flawless.

"I don't know." He looked at the cabinet behind her, willing it to provide an answer. He cleared his throat and shifted his feet. "Maybe we could get together for, uh, dinner or, I don't know, coffee?" He glanced at her, blatant hope and longing in his eyes.

Ashleigh smiled. It must be difficult to be a man and have to do the hard work of making the first move. "That's a very nice offer, Henry, but I guess I'm sort of seeing someone." She hated to admit it, even to herself, but if she agreed to a date with Henry, it would be a betrayal of whatever she and Nick had going on.

Henry's baleful expression changed to an angry scowl. "Is it that marine?"

"Yes," Ashleigh said. Her inner alarm bells were ringing, but she didn't know why. Henry was as harmless as a fly. Wasn't he?

"He's not good enough for you," Henry said.

"I don't think my personal life is any of your business, Henry." She shifted toward the door, checking the distance.

"Of course it is," Henry said. "How can you say it's not with all that's between us?"

"We have a working relationship," Ashleigh said as she began edging toward the door.

"Working relationship?" Henry thundered. The change in him was dramatic. Gone was the mild-mannered doctoral candidate, and in his place was an enraged man now stalking toward her.

"Henry, stop," Ashleigh said, infusing her voice with authority. He stopped advancing, but his anger didn't dissipate. He was still panting with, practically foaming at the mouth. Ashleigh should have turned and fled the house then, but she was rooted to the spot, bound by fear.

"You little piece of trash," Henry said between gritted teeth. "I was willing to make an exception for you, to lower my standards because I thought you were smart despite your lack of education. But I was wrong in the worst possible way. You're nothing. You're one step up from being a migrant worker in some field. Now get out of my house, and don't come back."

Ashleigh didn't have to be asked twice. She spun on her heel and darted away. Her hands shook as she made the long drive home. How had she been so wrong about Henry? He had seemed like a mild-mannered geek, but he was as much of a bully as Charlie had been. If she hadn't stood her ground when he was advancing on her, would he have hit her? If he found someone weaker, someone he could prey on, would he turn as abusive as Charlie? Why hadn't she stood up to his verbal attack? That one was easy to answer: his mercurial mood shift had reminded her too much of Charlie, and she panicked.

Nick was sitting on the front porch step when she arrived home. He stood as she approached, brushing the dust from the back of his pants. "What's wrong? Did something else happen to you?"

She had tried to smooth out her expression on the long ride home; apparently it hadn't worked. She pasted on a smile. "Nothing. I'm fine." Easing by him, she opened the front door and headed toward the bathroom so she could shower. Nick followed. He entered the bathroom and closed the door.

"Nick," she exclaimed. "I'm getting ready to shower here."

"Not until you tell me what has you so upset. Did you get another letter?"

She looked away, biting her lip. "I got a little upset at work. It's no big deal. The job is done."

"Did he refuse to pay you?" Nick asked.

"No, I have my money." She withdrew the envelope of cash and tossed it on the counter. Good thing he hadn't given her a check. He would no doubt stop payment on it now if he had.

"Ashleigh, what did he do to you? Did he hurt you?" His hand slid along her jaw and tilted her eyes up to meet his.

"He said some things, that was all. Just words. But he scared me. He was so angry. I…I misjudged him."

"He reminded you of Charlie," Nick guessed.

Ashleigh nodded.

"You're trembling." His arms slid around her. She leaned in, pressing her face to his chest as her arms slid around his waist. He was so solid, so secure. "Do you want me to rip off his arms and make him eat them?"

She laughed, the sound muffled by his shirt. "No. It wasn't that bad. I mean it was odd to see him switch gears like that. Normally I probably would have yelled at him for being such a rude bigot, but it triggered the old memories, and so I fled. I'm not proud of that."

"You did the right thing," Nick said.

"I did the cowardly thing."

"You're too brave for your own good sometimes," Nick said. He shuddered to think of the trouble she could get into, had already gotten into. And yet it was that bravery that attracted him to her. His hand smoothed up and down her back. She gave a sigh of contentment and nestled closer, and then she froze and stepped back, staring up at him in stunned surprise.

"What is it?" he asked.

"You did it," she blurted.

"Did what?" Was she angry at him? What had he done that was so wrong?

"You wore down my defenses, so sneakily I didn't even know it was happening. You got close to me. You made me fall in love with you."

She said the last part like an accusation. "About that, we need to talk."

"I have to take a shower." She leaned even farther away, putting as much distance between them as was possible in the small space.

"Later then," he insisted.

"I'll think about it," she said. She was really frowning now, her brows drawn together in annoyance. Nick's answering smile was probably smug, but how could he help it? The first part of his plan had worked better than he hoped.

"You're not allowed to be mad at me for this. Not my fault you fell for me."

"It is," she said. "You charmed me. You wooed me. You took me *dancing.*" She jabbed her finger in his chest, and he grinned unrepentantly.

"If you think the wooing is over, you are sadly mistaken," he said.

"What else is there?" she asked.

"It starts with this," he said. He pulled her close and kissed her. This kiss was different than the chaste pecks he had bestowed all week. This one was full of everything he was feeling, all the sparking, explosive attraction between them, and she returned it, her arms curling around his neck as she clung, one leg hitching up to curl around his waist, at least until a heavy knock sounded on the door.

"Ashleigh? Everything okay in there?" her father asked.

They froze, blinking dazedly as if being yanked from a deep sleep.

"Your dad is a living, breathing chastity belt," Nick whispered, disentangling himself from her snaring embrace.

"How else do you think I'm a twenty two year old virgin?" Ashleigh whispered. Out loud she replied, "It's fine, Dad. Nick and I were having a conversation, but it's over now."

"It's far from over," Nick said. "It's only just begun."

"So you say," Ashleigh said. She opened the bathroom door and shoved him outside.

$\mathcal{N}$ick landed on the other side of the bathroom door and saw Ashleigh's father still waiting for him to come out. He hadn't been there when Nick arrived at the house. If he had, there was a good chance Nick might not have followed Ashleigh to the bathroom. The women he dated didn't usually have fathers who cared about them. He wondered if it was one of the things that made Ashleigh so different from the others—a good reminder for his future children. Without a doubt he knew when he had daughters he wanted them to turn out like Ashleigh and not like any of the other scores of women he had been with. On that note…

"Reverend Desmond, may I talk to you a minute, please?" Nick asked.

The pastor turned and led the way to his study—a small room crammed to overflowing with a desk and dozens of books on theology, as well as the entire Harry Potter series. Interesting. Nick sat on one chair while the reverend took the one behind his desk.

"How may I help you today, Nick?" It was clear by his crisp, professional tone he was hoping Nick wanted to talk business or his immortal soul or anything besides his daughter. Nick decided to dispel that notion right away.

"It's about Ashleigh, sir."

The pastor's eyebrows drew together ever so slightly as he leaned forward, gripping his hands together on the desk. Nick wondered if it was a vain attempt to keep himself from throttling the marine across the table. "What about her?"

"About my future, our future. I thought it was time I informed you of my intentions where she is concerned." He tried not to look as nervous as he felt. Despite his vast experience with women, this was his first experience with a father, and he intended it to be his last. As such, he had to do it right; he had to be straightforward and put his cards on the table. "I thought it fair to warn you I have forever on my mind."

The reverend blinked, his hands gripping tighter. He paused for what felt like forever before he cleared his throat and plunged in. "I suppose I'm wondering what forever means to you, Nick. In this family we take commitment seriously. Ashleigh's mother and I have never mentioned divorce, not even in jest. Marriage vows are sacred, not something to be taken lightly or without thought." He delivered the missive in a grave voice one might use to tell a child a ghost story at a campout, but Nick was undeterred.

"Yes, sir, I understand. I know my appearance may not give you confidence of that, and my shoddy past as well as my unorthodox upbringing don't win me any points. I would tell you I've changed, but I don't think I have. I think this is who I've been all along and it took meeting Ashleigh to make me realize." He shifted, trying to think of the best way to explain. "I became a marine because I thought it would save me from being a bum. I thought they changed who I was by making me a responsible adult who values loyalty, integrity, and hard work. But they didn't change me—they allowed me to be who I had always been, to tap the man hidden inside the boy. That's what Ashleigh has done. I'm not changing for her. I'm becoming who I was always meant to be. I love her, and all I ask is the chance to prove myself worthy of your blessing."

There was another of those terrifyingly long pauses before he spoke. He stared at Nick. Nick had the uncomfortable feeling the man was peering at his inmost soul, but he resisted the urge to squirm. At last the pastor sighed and spoke. "I like you, Nick. I tried, really tried, not to. You have to understand how it is to be the father of two daughters. I can't afford to make a mistake, and I already made a mistake with Charlie." His voice broke. He glanced away and cleared his throat. "I take that failure seriously, but I also trust Ashleigh's judgment. And I trust my judgment. But we've both been wrong before. It's not fair, but you're going to have to pay for the sins of another man."

Nick's heart sank. Was he denying his blessing?

"This is one of those times when it's terrible to be a father because, despite everything, I'm going to say yes. I know my daughter. Saying no at this point would hurt her more than it would help. But I'll be watching you, Nick, even when it seems like I'm not. And if I see you take one step out of line, I won't go to the marines. I'll handle it myself. Do you understand me, son?"

Few times in Nick's adult life had he felt afraid of another man; this was one. He might be able to take the reverend in a fight, but a father's love for his daughter would add a level of ferocity that Nick was unaccustomed to. "Yes, sir," he said. "I won't let you down."

"See that you don't," the older man said. Then he stuck out his hand with a pleasant smile, as if they hadn't just had a terrifying conversation. Nick shook his hand and stumbled out of the office, sweating profusely. He didn't think he had ever been that nervous, even before his first kill. After all, he had been trained to shoot. No one had prepared him for what he'd just endured. But it was over. Now all he had to do was find Ashleigh and convince her he was worth the risk. He lingered by the office wall, taking a deep breath as his anxiety started all over again.

ASHLEIGH EMERGED from the shower to find the guests had already arrived. Kelsey, Lolly, and Ashton rode together while Melly drove separately. She hurried forth, embarrassed at having been caught unawares. She glanced around the room, searching for Nick, but he was nowhere in sight.

"Hey, y'all," Ashleigh said. She tried to sound friendly and welcoming despite her nerves. Normally she wasn't one to care if people didn't like her, but she knew Kelsey and Ashton were like brothers to Nick. She wanted them to like her, to approve of her, much more than she would admit to herself. "I'm sorry I'm late. I guess I got caught up staring at myself in the mirror."

"You're not late. We're early," Melly explained. "Sorry about that, we had some mix up with delivering Truck's car to the mechanic. I thought I was supposed to give him a ride, and they thought they were supposed to give him a ride, so we all showed up, and here we are." Melly smiled, and Ashleigh's anxiety inched down a notch. Melly was such a sweet and loving person, like her brother who stood at her side, bestowing a similarly gentle smile.

"Hey, Ashleigh," he said.

"Hey," Ashleigh replied.

"Hey," Kelsey said, imitating her drawl.

Her smile faltered, not sure if he was making fun of her. "Hey," Ashleigh said, her voice losing some of its enthusiasm.

"You're doing it wrong," Truck said to Kelsey. "You have to make the *e* more of an *a* sound. Let me demonstrate." He turned to Ashleigh. "Hey, how y'all doin'?" He sounded like a local. She had caught hints of an accent from him before. She smiled, realizing this was his olive branch.

"And where do y'all hail from?" she asked.

"Honey, I'm from somewhere so deep in South Carolina we consider y'all up here to be Yankees."

"Okay, you have to stop before the dueling banjos begin," Kelsey said.

"You're just jealous because you're not from the south like we are," Melly said.

"What are you talking about? You're from California like me," Kelsey said.

"*Southern* California," Melly amended. "You're from the north. You wouldn't understand unless you're from our latitude." She pointed between herself, Ashleigh, and Truck. She was clearly baiting Kelsey, and it appeared to be working.

"That's not fair," Kelsey replied. "We're from California. That's our club. You can't join their club."

Melly stood on her toes so she could press her palms to his cheeks. "You're forever five."

"Good thing you teach kindergarten," he replied, leaning forward to bestow a kiss onto her forehead.

Caleigh arrived home from school. She was finishing her senior year and bounced into the room looking fresh and beautiful. She was one of those extroverted people who lit the room by walking into it.

"Well, hello," Kelsey muttered, turning his attention and a beaming smile on Caleigh.

"She's eighteen," Melly said.

He lost his smile. "I'm officially a dirty old man. I didn't think it would happen this soon."

"It happened years ago," Melly said. "You're finally admitting it."

"Low," Kelsey said.

There was one person in the room who wasn't put off by Caleigh's age. Lolly peeked out from around Kelsey like a shy toddler peering from behind his mother's skirts. She noticed him and stopped short, blinking in surprise. Kelsey opened his mouth to comment, but Melly shook her head and he closed it. The other inhabitants of the room made awkward conversation while pretending not to notice Lolly working up his courage to approach Caleigh. Ashleigh made the introductions to her sister, using the opportunity to assess everyone and buy Lolly some time to gather his courage.

"This is Kelsey." It was hard not to add a flourish when introducing Kelsey. Like a peacock, his looks were so astounding they automatically drew all eyes toward him. Ashleigh thought it a mark of wisdom on her sister's part she discounted him as either being too old or too Kelsey for her because she seemed unfazed by his sandy blond hair and startlingly blue eyes. Ashleigh hadn't known he was from California, but she should have guessed. He looked like an extra from a fifties beach movie, someone who would be named "Moondoggie" and challenge Frankie Avalon for Annette Funicello.

"You've already met Melly," Ashleigh said. Melly had come over for supper twice while the men were away. She fit into the family like a third daughter; Ashleigh's parents had already adopted her as such and, though Melly wasn't one to wear her heart on her sleeve, Ashleigh knew she was pleased by the ready acceptance.

"This is Ashton," she continued. Ashton was handsome in his own right. His hair and eyes were brown like Nick's, but that was where the resemblance ended. Nick's features spoke of a Mediterranean heritage. His skin was olive-toned, his nose a little too large and slightly hooked, his face so stubbly he probably had to shave twice a day to keep his clean-cut appearance. He was swarthy and—dare she admit it—sexy. Realizing the path her thoughts were taking about Nick, she pulled them back and dwelled on Ashton as he made polite conversation with Caleigh. He was more Anglo-Saxon in appearance. Though he was tall, his features were small, his eyes deep set, his nose small and straight. He looked like someone who should have long hair, ride a horse, wear a velvet jacket, and adorn the cover of a regency novel.

"And this is…" Ashleigh paused when she reached Lolly, not sure how best to introduce him. Which would he prefer, his nickname or his real name?

"Lolly," he supplied. His voice was soft and shy. Caleigh smiled, dimpling. Ashleigh tried to see him through her sister's eyes. He was an interesting mix of softness and strength—big black eyes framed by what looked like thousands of long lashes, while his body, though small and compact, was solid steel.

"Hi," Caleigh said, holding out her hand for him to shake. Ashleigh's heart went out to Lolly. He was so shy, but it was obvious he was trying hard to think of something to say. Caleigh, too, seemed to be waiting for him to say something, anything. In fact it was as if the entire room was holding its breath.

Lolly took a deep breath and plunged in. "I was reading in the book of numbers, and I realized I don't have yours."

There was a second of stunned surprise. Lolly's face turned crimson. Caleigh laughed and pressed her hand over her lips to try and hold it back.

"That's it?" Kelsey said. "You wait for twenty three years and that's what you come up with?"

Lolly looked like he wished the floor would swallow him whole.

"Shh, Malibu Barbie," Caleigh said, poking Kelsey. "I liked it." She smiled at Lolly and he blinked at her, dazzled, not knowing quite where to go next.

"Did she make fun of my California good looks?" Kelsey asked.

"I believe she did," Truck said. His tone radiated approval.

"What is wrong with the women in this family?" Kelsey asked.

"They're wise beyond their years," Melly said.

"Melly, you never take my side," Kelsey pouted.

"I take your side every time you're right, Kelsey. So, I guess you're correct—never."

He reached out and drew her into a loose chokehold. "Someday I'm going to astound you with my depth and sensitivity."

"Today?" she asked, clasping her arms comfortably around his waist. They shared a look, and Kelsey sighed.

"Yes, today. Hey, PK," he addressed Ashleigh. "I'm sorry about the Tisha thing. I was wrong to try and interfere. I'll probably do it again, just so you know. But it's clear you have sunk your innocent little kitten claws deep into Nick's heart. I hope you're miserably happy and have lots of little Amish babies I can spoil with my talk of moving pictures and rock-n-roll devil music." He touched his finger to her forehead as if bestowing a blessing, and Melly gave him a squeeze around his middle.

"Oh, um, thank you," Ashleigh said. She wasn't often at a loss for words, but Kelsey had her on the ropes. How was she supposed to reply to that? She looked around, hoping to find a reprieve, and found Nick stalking toward her, an unreadable smile on his face.

"Is Kelsey torturing you?" he asked. His arm slid possessively around her waist.

"No more than usual," Ashleigh replied. The feeling of belonging was almost overwhelming.

"What?" Kelsey asked, feigning innocence. "I simply mentioned marriage and children to your girlfriend of a week. What is weird about that? If your relationship can't handle the pressure, maybe you need to rethink things."

"It can handle it," Nick said. Ashleigh gave an uncomfortable chuckle and eased away, shooting Melly a look of desperation.

"*Whoa,*" Melly mouthed.

"*I know,*" Ashleigh mouthed back as her mother called them to supper. She had prepared mounds of fried chicken, potato salad, biscuits, and green beans. After seeing how much the guys ate when she cooked for them, she hoped it would be enough.

Lolly held Caleigh's chair. She issued forth another smile that caused him to blush. Ashleigh approved at the match. They were both years behind their peers in terms of innocence and experience. Their temperaments would be well-matched, too, though she supposed she was putting the cart ahead of the horse. They seemed to be taking baby steps toward getting to know each other. Plus there was the issue of their age difference. Lolly, though shy and sweet, was still five years older. Caleigh was in high school, if only for a few more weeks. Ashleigh thought her dad's head would probably pop off if another of his daughters tried to date a marine at this point.

Nick was quiet during dinner, thoughtful, as conversation swirled around them. Ashley was reserved, too, as she replayed the ugly scene with Henry in her head, wishing she had handled it differently. Before she knew it, the meal ended and it was time for pie. She stood to help serve, but her mother shooed her away. Nick leaned over to whisper in her ear.

"Do you think maybe we could slip out and have that talk now?"

"Okay," Ashleigh whispered through lips suddenly stiff and dry. The week had lulled her into a false sense of security. She had hoped they were slipping naturally into a relationship, but Nick still wanted to have *the talk.* Wasn't it supposed to be the woman who wanted to define the relationship while the man ran away screaming? Why was

Mr. I've-dated-a-thousand-women so anxious to label what was between them?

As soon as they stepped out onto the porch, he let her know. Ashleigh backed against the wall and tucked her hands behind her back. Her knuckles rasped against the bricks and she pressed closer, seeking reassurance from the rough clay.

"Here's the thing, Ash," Nick began. He stood beside her. One of his hands was pressed against the bricks. She wondered if he needed the support when he finally said what it was he had brought her out here to reveal. "I'm going to marry you."

There was a noise. Ashleigh was in such a state of shock she thought maybe it was her brain exploding, but then she was in Nick's arms and he was propelling her toward the house. He opened the door and shoved her roughly inside. She turned to ask him what happened, but he wasn't there.

The noise must have been louder than she thought because everyone tumbled from the dining room into the living room and stopped short, staring at her. "Ashleigh, what happened?" her father asked.

Time began to slow, and Ashleigh began to think rationally again. The popping sound started to make sense as she replayed it in her head. "I think someone tried to shoot me."

CHAPTER 21

Several things happened at once. Kelsey, Lolly, and Truck streamed past her, practically knocking her into the wall in their haste to get outside.

"Don't eat my pie, Luscious," Kelsey called toward Melly before he threw open the door and disappeared into the night.

Ashleigh's mother and sister burst into hysterical weeping. Her father and Melly rushed forward, each taking one of Ashleigh's arms as they ushered her toward the windowless dining room. Everyone sat. No one said a word, but it was far from peaceful because Mrs. Desmond and Caleigh were seeing who could out weep each other, or so it seemed to Ashleigh. She cast a plaintive look toward her father.

"Come on, let's go into the kitchen and clean up," he suggested, herding the two hysterical females to the other room. Ashleigh let out a breath she didn't know she had been holding. Usually she and her father worked as a team to keep the others calm, but she lacked the energy to do her part today. She was out of reassurances for the moment. The ensuing silence was a blessed relief, broken only by the sound of Kelsey's fork scraping plate as Melly polished off the rest of his pie.

"I'm not even hungry," Melly said when she saw Ashleigh watching. "I can't resist doing something when he tells me not to."

"He calls you Luscious," Ashleigh said, which was an odd thing to focus on at the moment.

Melly shrugged one shoulder. "I hate it, but I have to pretend I don't care or he'll do it more. Sometimes I feel like his mom." She gave the remaining bit of crust a vicious stab.

"Nick said he's going to marry me."

The fork clattered to the plate. "Oh, wow. You win. What did you say?"

"Nothing. The shot went off, and Nick herded me into the house." She swiveled in her chair, staring worriedly toward the front. "Shouldn't we call the police?"

"No offense to the local cops, but our guys are better. Let them do their stuff and *then* we'll call the police," Melly replied.

Ashleigh drummed her fingers on the table. "Don't you ever worry about them when they're working?"

"I wouldn't be normal if I didn't. But after you say goodbye and then see them return safely so many times, it gets better. It begins to feel routine."

"I think Ashton likes you," Ashleigh blurted. Her mind was a carousel of revolving topics as she tried to settle on one that didn't make her feel like she was about to jump out of her skin. She had noticed Ashton's eyes stray toward Melly more than once that evening, a soft, open look on his usually cool and impassive face.

Melly laughed and shook her head. "Nah. Truck's not one to expand his circle easily. I think he's still asking himself how I managed to sneak by and become friends with him."

Ashleigh wasn't so sure, but for all their sakes she hoped Melly was right. Love triangles and friendship didn't go well. Not that Melly would admit there was anything between her and Kelsey, either. Maybe the real problem was Melly and her denial. Did she not under-stand how men were drawn to her exotic beauty? It was a wonder Nick was somehow immune. She glanced toward the door again.

"Ashleigh, relax. You have no idea how good our guys are."

Our guys. The phrase made something flutter in Ashleigh's chest.

Outside her family she had never belonged to anyone before, preferring instead to remain a loner. Now she had somehow become part of this team. Even Kelsey and Truck, though begrudging, had finally given their approval. Could she really do this? Could she not only someday marry Nick, but marry his team? Because that's what her life would entail. He wasn't alone—he was a package deal. And she would only have him part time. She had no illusions about his job. It was dangerous, and it kept him away for more than half the year.

But maybe spending so many years as a loner had prepared her for the life she was now contemplating. She wasn't one of those women who needed constant contact and reassurance. She knew how to do everything for herself, even all the mechanical repairs husbands typically handled. In addition to repair work, she had a head for finances. She could run a household completely on her own, something other men had found intimidating.

She started to laugh. Melly looked at her like she was crazy, but how could she explain? She had spent her life feeling like a freak because she didn't fit in. And now she had finally found her niche with a marine whose life bore no resemblance to her own. Yet somehow they fit perfectly together. Nick with supreme confidence in his masculinity and long absences was the perfect partner for her take-no-prisoners independent nature. He not only wouldn't mind if she took charge of the finances and fixed the plumbing, he would require it because he wouldn't be there to do it himself. Never in a million years would she have pictured herself with someone like him, but now he was here she couldn't picture herself with anyone else. Of course she had to marry Nick. Who else?

"Are you having some sort of breakdown?" Melly asked, leaning forward to study Ashleigh's face with genuine concern.

Ashleigh shook her head and wiped her streaming eyes. "Maybe. It's been a crazy few weeks. It feels like the good kind of breakdown, though."

"I didn't know there was a good kind," Melly said.

"Definitely," Ashleigh said. "Life is funny sometimes in the way it works out. Don't you think?"

"I haven't found much hilarity yet," Melly said. "Maybe because I've never been in love."

The front door opened. Despite Melly's calm demeanor, she scurried into the living room as quickly as Ashleigh. They arrived together and saw Lolly with Tisha, her arm twisted behind her back as he held her in a death grip.

"Oh," was all Ashleigh could muster. She felt like someone had punched her in the gut. Tisha was trying hard to look angry, but too much fear was showing through.

"Tisha," Melly said it like a question.

"I found the weapon on her," Lolly said. "It's a safe bet she placed the bomb and sent the letter, too."

"You can't prove anything," Tisha said, trying and failing to wrench out of his clutch.

"I don't have to," Lolly said. "But you might want to get a lawyer when you talk to the police."

She shuddered and sniffled. Ashleigh felt wretched, both for the other woman and for herself. She was partially to blame for this mess.

Nick and Kelsey walked in, followed closely by Truck. Nick looked as shocked and stricken as Ashleigh felt. There was a moment of stunned silence until Kelsey reached the dining room and yelled, "Woman, you ate my pie!"

"Tish," Nick said. His voice was full of pain and accusation. "Why?"

"Why do you think?" Tisha asked. This time she finally wrenched free of Lolly, or he simply let her go. She whirled to face Nick, and he flinched at her rage-filled expression. "I thought we had something real. I thought we were forever. And then you dump me for her. You said you were going to marry her." Fat, sloppy tears began to slip quietly down her cheeks. Kelsey edged into the room and hovered behind Melly. Ashleigh wondered if maybe he thought there would be more violence.

"I'm sorry," Nick said. "I never meant to hurt you. But even if I did, that's no reason to try and kill Ashleigh."

"I wasn't trying to kill her," Tisha said. "I was so angry, and it hurt so much." She swiped the back of her hand across her dripping nose.

"She has everything, and I have nothing. I wanted to make her hurt a little, to feel some of the pain I was feeling."

"I'm sorry," this time it was Ashleigh who spoke. She took a step forward, arm outstretched, and then dropped it before she could reach her target. Touching Tisha didn't seem like a good idea. She looked like a wild animal caught in a trap, waiting for a hand to bite. "I'm really sorry, Tisha. What I did was wrong. I should never have spent so much time with Nick when he was yours. There's no justification for it, and I'm sorry. Truly."

Tisha blinked at her in surprise. Clearly an apology was the last thing she expected. Truck reached the end of his emotional tolerance. "Are we ready to call the cops here?" He pulled out his phone.

"No," Nick and Ashleigh said together.

"I don't want her to go to jail," Ashleigh said.

"Neither do I," Nick said.

"You're kidding, right?" Truck said. "She sent a threatening letter, made and planted a bomb, and took a shot at Ashleigh. In what universe would we let her go?"

The one where I don't want to start our relationship under a burden of guilt or ugliness, Ashleigh thought. She glanced at Nick and knew he was thinking the same thing. They wanted to put this behind them, not only for themselves but for Tisha, too. They had hurt her and weren't completely blameless in the situation.

"Hello," Truck pressed. "Felon in the middle of the room. Anybody gonna back me up here?"

Lolly was always on the side of the underdog and didn't say a word. Kelsey opened his mouth, but Melly elbowed him in the ribs, and he shut it. Ashleigh glanced at her parents hovering at the edge of the room. They seemed to be deferring to her for once, or they simply agreed with her.

"Y'all are crazy," Truck said. He stormed by them and into the dining room.

"You won't do it again, will you?" Ashleigh asked Tisha.

Tisha shook her head. To her credit, she looked subdued and penitent. Though she didn't quite manage to eke out an apology.

"I'll take her home," Lolly volunteered. Melly tossed him her keys before Kelsey tugged her into the dining room. "Explain my missing pie, Senorita," he said as they disappeared into the other room. Ashleigh's parents faded back into the kitchen where the sound of clinking glassware resumed once again.

Lolly and Tisha left, and then it was Nick and Ashleigh, still staring across the room at each other. "And they say committed relationships are boring," Nick said. He began making his way to Ashleigh.

"About that," Ashleigh said as she advanced toward him, stopping short of reaching him in the middle of the room. "You can't tell me we're getting married. Don't I have a say in the matter?"

"Nope," Nick said. "We've already proved your judgment is lousy when it comes to me. You're putty in my hands. Face it; I did us both a favor by making the decision for you."

She shook her head. "That's not how it works."

"What if I throw in a bargaining chip?" he suggested.

"Like what?" she asked.

"Marry me, and I'll go to Officer Candidate School."

She could no longer stay away from him. She closed the small gap between them by throwing her arms around his neck. "Nick, do you mean it?"

He nodded. "I want this, Ash; I want it all. I'm crazy filled up with ambition right now. I want the house, the career, the kids. Let's buy a minivan." He rested his forehead on hers, his eyes crinkling at the corners as he smiled.

"Pull back, Mister, I have a bargaining chip of my own."

"Somehow I figured you would," he said. "Let's hear it."

"I plan on wearing white to our wedding, if you know what I mean," she said. He groaned, and she patted his chest. "You'll make it," she reassured him.

"We're going to have to take your dad on all our dates."

"About that," she added, taking a deep breath. "You know this is the south, and we're a traditional family. You're going to have to talk to him. You're going to have to get his approval."

"About that," he said, "there's something I have to tell you. I already did."

Ashleigh let out a little yelp, the most girlish sound she had ever made in her life, as she stood on her toes and kissed him breathless.

* * *

IN THE DINING ROOM, Melly sat on Kelsey's lap, feeding him a reserved piece of pie while Truck sat beside them, staring sullenly at the opposing wall. They turned toward the dining room when they heard Ashleigh's squeal of surprised delight.

"What do you suppose that's about?" Melly asked.

"Maybe they're washing each other's feet or taking communion," Kelsey suggested.

"Maybe they're just crazy. Everyone here is crazy," Truck said.

"Better run, Ashton, before the happiness starts to leach into your system," Melly teased. "You might find yourself smiling one of these days."

"I smile at *you*," Ashton said, bestowing her with a flirtatious smile that made Kelsey frown and shift her possessively away.

"I'm with Truck on this one," he said. "These people are messed up. No one is this happy and well-settled. It's giving me the creeps."

"You're feeling threatened because Nick's in love and moving on," Melly said.

"Moving on," Kelsey repeated. "He's not moving on; he's dating someone new. No woman will come between us. Between any of us."

"That's right," Truck agreed. "Women aren't worth it."

"Good thing there isn't one in this room who might take offense," Melly said.

"Obviously you're the exclusion to all talk about women, Melly," Kelsey said. "On account of you not really being one."

"Sometimes my life makes me sad," Melly mused.

"Join the club," Truck said.

"What are you talking about? Life is good," Kelsey said.

"That's because there's a beautiful woman in your lap feeding you pie. But someday the woman and the pie will be gone, and then where will you be?" Truck said. "Alone and miserable like the rest of us."

"Melly will never leave me," Kelsey said. He wrapped his arms around her waist and gave her a squeeze. "Will you, Mel?"

"The very moment something better comes along," Melly said cheerfully. "Maybe before then."

"You're mean," Kelsey said.

"Are you promising her your eternal devotion?" Truck asked.

"Pfft. No," Kelsey said.

"Good thing you're pretty," Melly said. "It almost makes up for your total lack of depth."

"Almost," Truck added.

"Like you're so deep," Kelsey said.

"I'm an iceberg," Truck said. No one had any reply to that because it was probably true.

Nick and Ashleigh entered the room, Lolly following close behind. Caleigh filtered in from the kitchen as if she had been waiting and watching for him. He held her chair again as she sat down. She smiled, and he returned it, his cheeks an adorable shade of pink.

A peaceful silence settled around the table, at least until Kelsey spoke.

"PK, what are the chances your mom might make us another pie?"

As if in answer to his question, Mrs. Desmond appeared—pie in hand. "I had another pie in reserve. I know how you boys like to eat." She set it on the table with a flourish and disappeared back into the kitchen.

"I think I could begin to really like it here," Kelsey said.

"Me, too," Lolly agreed.

"Me, too," Truck added. Everyone glanced at him in surprise. "What? They have pie."

Melly held her pie-laden fork aloft. "To the toughest marines I know who can also be bought with pie."

"Hear, hear," the guys agreed, then lapsed into silence again as they quietly ate their pie.

Thank you for reading *Shooter,* the first book in the Brothers Courageous series. For more books, please check out my website at www.vanessagraybartal.com.